THE VENUS DEATH

THE
VENUS DEATH

by

BEN BENSON

WILDSIDE PRESS

The Venus Death

Published by Wildside Press LLC
wildsidepress.com | bcmystery.com

AUTHOR'S NOTE _____

MY many thanks to my friends and technical advisers at General Headquarters, Massachusetts State Police, Boston:

Colonel Daniel I. Murphy, former Commissioner of Public Safety

Lieutenant George F. Roche

Lieutenant Joseph P. McEnaney

S.O. Sergeant John F. Collins

Also, for their warm hospitality, my thanks to the officers and men at Troop A Headquarters, Framingham, Mass., The State Police Training School and the Andover Barracks.

THE VENUS DEATH

CHAPTER 1 _____

I first met her at a bar in Danford, Massachusetts. Usually, on my night off, I would drive directly home to Cambridge to see my mother and father. But this was one of those nights after a long, hard patrol. I was tired, and I thought just this one time I would go into nearby Danford, have a few beers, possibly take in a movie, and go back to the barracks and get some sleep.

The bar was on Berkshire Street, downtown in the city. There was nothing ornate or pretentious about it. It had the usual long counter, the mirror and array of bottles behind it. A half-dozen booths, a television set and a jukebox.

I was there early, just after six. The counter was empty and there were only two people in the booths. I sat on a leather-topped stool, my elbows on the bar, twisting the second glass of beer in my hands. The bartender, a small, ferret-faced man, was paying no attention to me. I think he knew, with a bartender's shrewd instinct, that I wasn't a drinker or a spender, that I was only there to kill a little time. He was moving some bottles around in back of the counter when suddenly he stopped and turned toward the door. I couldn't help but turn and look, too. A girl had come in.

She was about twenty-one years old and five feet five in her high-heeled black pumps. Her head was bare, her hair golden-yellow, soft and wavy and not cut short, but falling almost to her shoulders. Her skin was smooth and creamy, and her mouth was full and delicate and softly alluring, and she had a small perky nose with just enough tilt to it to make it provocative. She had a well-curved, full-hipped body and perfect nylon-sheathed legs. She was wearing a tailored gray flannel suit that snugged over her hips and thighs. She carried a large black leather shoulder bag and black gloves. She was the most beautiful girl I had ever seen.

I didn't want to stare at her so I turned back to my beer. It was foolish for me to look at her, anyway. I had a girl back home in Cambridge named Ellen.

I heard her heels click-click by me and an aura of tantalizing perfume wafted up and enveloped the sour smell of beer. Through the mirror I saw her sit down two stools away. She was looking at the price list on the wall. At the same time she was slowly peeling off her gloves. The bartender came and stood over her.

"I don't know," she said to him. "I don't know what I'll have. Perhaps an Old Fashioned."

Her voice was soft and throaty, with a little huskiness to it. I fidgeted with the button on my sports jacket, thinking she didn't belong in an obscure bar on Berkshire Street, but in a place more like the Onyx Room at the Hotel Dan-

2

ford Terrace. I lit a cigarette and I noticed my hand trembled a little. I knew I had no intention of picking her up, but she was beautiful and desirable, and her nearness sent my blood quickening. I kept looking at her in the bar mirror and I saw her drink come. She took a bill from her bag and paid for it.

She picked up the short, stubby glass. She sipped at it. Then she coughed and reached quickly for a white lacy handkerchief. The bartender came over to her.

"Anything wrong, ma'am?" he asked.

"No," she said. "I swallowed it the wrong way. May I have a glass of water, please?"

The water came and she drank it. Then she fished in her bag again. Her head came up and turned toward me apologetically. She said, "I'm afraid I forgot to bring my cigarettes. Would you mind terribly?"

"No," I said. "Not at all." My hands were all thumbs as I took out the pack. I fumbled with them, dropped them on the floor and picked them up again. I reached over and handed her one. Then I lit it for her. She took one puff, without inhaling. Then she put the cigarette down in an oversized glass ash tray.

Suddenly she moved off her stool and sat down on the one next to me. "I hate to drink alone," she said.

"Everybody does," I said. "It's a universal complaint."

"I can say hello now. My name is Manette Venus." Then she smiled, showing small, white teeth.

"I'm Ralph Lindsey," I said. "Manette is a pretty name."

"Thanks. Do you come here often?"

"It's my first."

"Mine, too," she said. The cigarette burned in the ash

3

tray and her drink remained untouched. "When a girl gets lonely, she doesn't quite know what to do sometimes."

"*You* get lonely?"

Her thin eyebrows arched up. "Why not?"

"But anybody who looks like you—"

"You're sweet," she said. "But I *am* lonely and I've been lonely for a month—ever since I came to Danford. It's not a very cheery city."

"It's a mill town. You can't expect too much in a mill town."

"You live in Danford?"

"Not exactly. About five miles outside. On the turnpike."

"Do you work in one of the mills?"

"No."

"Then you're a college student. With those shoulders you must be on the football team."

"No, I'm a cop," I said. "A state trooper."

"A what?" she asked.

"A state trooper."

"Oh, how nice," she said. Then her voice brightened as she told me she had noticed the state troopers on the road, and how she had admired the handsome two-toned blue uniforms, and how one had stopped her once for a traffic violation.

"But he was very polite," she said.

"Thanks." I grinned. "We usually get more gripes than compliments."

She smiled. "He was very young, and you're very young, too."

"I'm twenty-three."

"And how long have you been a trooper?"

4

"Three months. I'm what they call a 'boot.' Another name for recruit or rookie."

"Your face is sunburnt and your nose is peeling. But you're very good-looking."

"Thanks," I said. "It's the outdoor life."

"That makes you good-looking?"

"No. I was talking about the sunburn."

Then she laughed and I grinned back at her and the air in the place seemed warmer and mellower and friendlier. She said, "I wonder if they serve food here."

"I wouldn't try it," I said. "But if you're hungry—"

"Oh, not really. I would like a lobster salad roll, though."

"You like lobster?"

"Love it. I come from Cleveland. Lobster is expensive there."

"We could go to Howard Johnson's. They have good lobster rolls."

She slid off her stool and picked up her bag and gloves. "If you'd like to take me," she said, "I'm ready."

"You haven't touched your drink," I reminded her.

"I don't care for it," she said hurriedly. Then, as the bartender stared at her, she touched my elbow.

We went to the door. My car was outside. It was a 1946 Ford coupé. The fenders were battered but it had a good motor. We got in and I drove out the turnpike to the nearest Howard Johnson's.

It was as simple as that.

The lobster salad rolls and coffee had come and gone. She refused a cigarette. I sat across from her in the booth, looking at her face in the glow of the table lamp. Her face was finely shaped, delicately boned, but inexpressive

5

and immobile. Her eyes were heavily lidded and long-lashed, and their color was like the deep blue of the Gulf Stream. I don't know what she was thinking. But I knew what *I* was thinking, and I had a twinge of conscience about it. It was of Ellen back home in Cambridge, to whom I was engaged. Also, I was thinking of fate, and how it was just plain luck the way I had met Manette Venus. You didn't meet girls like her very often and it would never happen again. And unconsciously I must have said it out loud.

"What was that?" she asked.

"Pure luck," I said. "The way we met, I mean. My father always said life is ninety per cent luck, but people don't recognize it. Only the smart ones do, and they take advantage of it."

"Is your father one of the smart ones?"

"No," I said. "Not that smart." I didn't tell her my father had no luck at all. He had been a state trooper who, in 1939, had been shot in the back and had been paralyzed from the waist down ever since. "Are *you* one of the smart ones?"

She laughed. "Me neither. You see, *I* work in the mill."

"You? Which one?"

"Staley Woolen. Out in Staleyville. I'm in the office. Clerical work."

"It's a big mill. I go by there in a cruiser every Friday. It's on one of my patrols."

"I've never seen you."

"I go by before noon. I guess everybody's inside then."

"Are you alone in the car?"

"Yes."

6

"I've never noticed you," she said. "Lots of times I look out the window."

"I'll slow down the next time," I said. Then I told her how she couldn't miss the cruiser. It was pale blue. The state seals were on the doors and there were big white letters on the rear deck that said *Massachusetts State Police*. And on top of the roof there was a red light and a siren.

"I'll surely watch for it Friday," she said. "I'll wave to you from the window." Then she smiled. "But Friday's a long way off, and the evening is still young. Of course, if you've made other arrangements—"

"No," I said. "What would you like to do?"

"Anything you say. I don't care."

"We could take in a movie. There's a drive-in about a mile down the pike."

"I'd love to see a movie," she said.

We left Howard Johnson's. It had grown dark. I was crossing the parking lot with her when suddenly she stopped. She said, "Do you always carry a gun, Ralph?"

I turned to her. "What difference would that make?"

"I'm just curious," she said with a short, nervous laugh. "It isn't a secret or anything, is it?"

"No. Cops have to carry a gun at all times. I've got a little .38 Smith and Wesson Special here on my belt."

"Where?"

"At my right hip pocket." I opened my jacket and showed her the tiny leather open holster and the butt of the S&W.

She said, "No one would ever know. It doesn't show one bit, Ralph."

"That's supposed to be the general idea," I said.

7

We went to the drive-in theater. Now I like the movies. But if you asked me, I couldn't even tell you what the picture was that October night. I was looking at her as she sat beside me. Her face was tilted up toward the screen, her hands clasped primly in her lap, her profile finely etched. She was a strange girl. Before there had been a forced brashness in her, now she seemed shy and timid. She didn't seem to be too relaxed either, because every once in a while her foot would begin to tap on the rubber floor mat.

The picture ended and the lights went up. I started the car and we left the drive-in theater. I said, "How about a drink somewhere? A nightcap."

"I'm not much for drinking, Ralph. Thanks, but I think it's time to go home."

"Where do you live?"

"I don't want to trouble you. You can let me off downtown."

"It's no trouble," I said.

"I live on Glen Road. I have a room with a private family. You go down the turnpike, past the Blue Grotto, to the first set of lights. Turn left."

"You don't live with your folks?"

"No, I'm all alone in Danford."

I came to the lights and turned off. I drove along until I saw the sign *Glen Road*. On either side were curving streets with new houses. The houses began to thin out. I slowed down and looked at her.

"It's a little way ahead," she said.

There was a wooded area for half a mile with no houses at all. Then a light gleamed through the trees.

"There," she said.

8

I pulled over and stopped in front of it. The house stood alone. Two stories and a high gabled attic. The house was old Victorian, with rotting shingles and a tangled unkempt high hedge. It had diamond-patterned windows. On the lawn was an old-fashioned post lantern. It cast a weak yellow light.

"You're a long way from the bus," I said.

"Oh, no. The bus goes right by here to Staleyville. And the driver always stops at the house." She picked up her bag. She put it down again. Her hand reached for the door handle. She turned to me nervously.

"Well," she said. "I really have to go in."

"I hope to see you again some time."

She moved over in the seat, closer to me. "Don't you like me?" she asked suddenly.

"Why, sure, I like you," I said, startled. "I—"

She put her arms around my neck. I could feel the soft resiliency of her body, the cool, scented cheek and a tendril of blond hair. I felt her warm breath on my face.

"This is what I meant," she whispered. Her lips came to mine, hot and moist, clinging. She broke away, picked up her bag and pushed on the door handle.

"Wait a minute," I said, catching my breath. But she was out of the car. I slid across the seat and came out on the road beside her. I took her by the shoulders and turned her around. "I want to see you again, Manette."

"That's better," she said. "When?"

"Sunday," I said. "My first Sunday off since I was assigned to the troop."

"What time?"

"In the morning. I have the whole day."

"In the afternoon," she said.

9

"We'll have dinner together," I said. "Maybe I'd better phone you to make sure."

"You don't have to. But the number is Danford 6–1530. Do you have a pencil?"

"I don't need any. 6–1530. I'll remember it like my own badge number."

I went up the crumbling flagstone walk with her. The house windows were dark. She took a key from her bag and put it in the door lock.

"Until Sunday then," she said. "Good night, Ralph."

"Good night, Manette," I said.

She opened the door and stepped inside. The door closed. I stood there for a moment. Then I went back down the walk and got into my car. I looked at the house. A light had gone on upstairs. I saw her come to the window and draw the shade. I started up the car and drove back to the turnpike.

I drove steadily, not fast. She had left a perfumed scent in the car. I was staring at the road, but I was thinking of the strangeness of her actions. She was like no other girl I had ever known. She had told me nothing of herself. And the more I thought of it, the pickup at the bar didn't seem like plain luck. It was almost as if she had expected me. And while I was trying to figure things out I missed the blue neon sign that said *State Police*. I had to go along the turnpike to the next cutoff.

I drove back, crossed over, went around the arched driveway and into the rear parking area. I put the car away, went in through the garage and up to the first floor.

It was quiet in the barracks. I crossed the asphalt-tiled, antiseptic-smelling corridor. The guardroom was empty and the television screen was dark. The cellblock and its four cells stood open and vacant. In the communications room I saw the civilian dispatcher. The shortwave radio was mute, but I could hear the rhythmical clacking of the teletype machines.

I went into the office. The duty sergeant was Stan Maleski. He looked up at me from behind his desk. He wore the pale blue worsted uniform shirt with the dark blue sergeant stripes on the sleeves. The sleeves were sharply creased and at the right shoulder yoke was the State Police patch. His necktie was black silk and fastened to his shirt with the silver tie clip that carried the state shield on it.

"What are *you* doing in?" Maleski asked. "Didn't you go home?"

"No," I said, signing in. "I went to Danford and hung around."

Maleski stood up and went to the bulletin board. He put up a notice on the clip stand. He was carrying a short-barreled S&W revolver in a hip holster. His trousers were the dark blue uniform slacks with a broad stripe down the side.

I went over and looked at the bulletin board. "Quiet tonight?" I asked.

"Pretty quiet," he said. "There's coffee in the kitchen if you want it, Ralph."

"I'm restless enough as it is," I said. "Coffee would only make it worse, Stan."

He looked at me with puzzled eyes, his square jaw pushed to one side. Then the telephone on his desk rang. He went over and picked it up.

"State Police," he said. "Troop E Headquarters. Sergeant Maleski. Yes, sir . . ."

I left him and went upstairs to my room. It was a bare

room. It contained two narrow steel beds, a chest of drawers and a mirror and nothing else. I switched on the light. The bed near the window was mine. It was covered with a squared, taut, dark blue blanket, a white pillow and a six-inch border of the top sheet showing. In the other bed, next to the locked closet, was the huddled, blanketed form of Patrolman Philip Kerrigan. I went over and shook him. "Wake up," I said.

He groaned, twisted under the blanket and covered his head. Then his head poked out. He blinked his eyes. "What time is it?"

"Eleven o'clock," I said.

"Dammit," he said. "I just got in from a patrol and I've got another one at six A.M." He buried his head again.

I shook him once more. "I met a girl tonight, Phil."

"I thought you had a girl named Ellen," he mumbled.

"This is a little different," I said.

"I know. The other one is sixty miles away."

"A beautiful blonde," I said. "The most beautiful girl I ever met in my life. Her name is Manette Venus."

"Hurray for you," he grunted. "Now breeze off my ear and let me sleep."

"I'm going to see her again Sunday."

"That's just peachy," he said. Then he wrenched himself up on one elbow. One eye opened. He pushed his dark hair away from his forehead. "You tell her you're a trooper?"

"Sure."

"And she wants to see you again?"

"Sure."

"The girl's crazy," he said, subsiding again. "A real psycho."

"Listen," I said. "There's something funny about it. She

12

acted a little strange—" But his breathing had become deep and steady. I let him lie there. I went into the bathroom and washed up. Then I came back, undressed, locked my gun in the closet, and put out the light. I got into the hard narrow bed and lay there looking out across the dark fields. I could see the shortwave radio tower and the blinking red lights on top of it. I kept looking at them until I fell asleep.

CHAPTER 2 _____

SHE phoned me at the barracks the next evening, Thursday, just after I had come in from a larceny investigation. There was to be a Signal Nineteen, a gambling raid in Lincolnshire, and her call came in as we were getting ready.

She had a hauntingly husky voice over the telephone. She asked if I wanted to see her that evening. I told her I would have liked nothing better, but I was on duty. I did say I would ride by Staley Woolen the next morning before noon.

And I did, too. At 11:45 Friday morning I came off Route 138, moved down the valley and into Staleyville. I was driving cruiser 56, a new one, nicely polished and shiny, with a long buggy-whip antenna in the rear. I went past the old white church in the center of Staleyville, over the stone bridge and the mill dam, and onto the two-lane road that led to the factory. Ahead of me I could see the tall

14

smokestacks with their drifting gray plumes, and the moss-covered, ancient, red-brick buildings of the Staley Woolen Company. There was a tall, chain-link cyclone fence, the top of it carrying three strands of barbed wire. I came up slowly. An armored truck emerged from the gate and turned onto the road. As it passed me, the driver blew his horn twice and waved. I waved back. It meant the weekly payroll at Staley had been delivered without incident.

As I came to the gate, the guard walked out of his glassed-in booth. He was a gray old man in a gray old uniform. He grinned at me and shouted something I couldn't hear. I waved to him. I was driving by the factory in low gear, at three miles per hour. I looked up at the office building, a two-story structure directly inside the gate. The sun was high in the sky and the windows were shadowed. I didn't see her.

I went on ahead, turned onto Route 116 and finished my morning patrol. I kept thinking it was a long time until Sunday.

But I saw her before Sunday. On Saturday morning I had a routine traffic patrol. I moved out of the driveway of Troop E Headquarters and stopped at the turnpike to let the cars go by. I looked back at the wide, velvet-green lawn. In the center of it were the tall twin flagpoles, the American flag and the white-and-blue Commonwealth flag billowing out in the soft warm October breeze. Beyond was the red-brick Colonial barracks, the high steel radio tower behind it, the evergreen shrubs banked in front of it. I could feel the pleasantness of the warm sun on the back of my neck.

I turned the cruiser out onto the turnpike. Ahead of me a small gray convertible was parked on the shoulder of the road. Somebody inside it blew the horn three times. I passed it, stopped the cruiser, and walked back. I had already seen who was inside the car. It was Manette Venus and she was alone.

"Hi." I grinned at her. "I didn't know you had a car."

"It's not mine," she said. "I borrowed it from a friend."

"And I thought you had no friends in Danford."

"It belongs to a girl in my office. I don't work today and she let me borrow it for a few hours." Her eyes swept over me. "I've never seen you in uniform. You're positively striking. But isn't that an awfully big gun to be carrying? It's not the same as the other night."

"No, this is the regulation, long-barreled service revolver."

"And what's in that little black leather case on your belt? A hand grenade?"

I laughed. "No, my handcuffs."

"And that long leather pouch on your belt?"

"The ammunition carrier. It holds twenty-four rounds."

"All that? And do you carry a machine gun or a rifle in the car?"

"Sometimes."

"What do you keep in the trunk of the car?"

"A spare tire."

She made a face at me. "Everybody carries a spare tire. What else?"

"The two-way radio is in there. Also a folded emergency stretcher." I smiled at her. "Why so curious, Manette?"

"Does it bother you, Ralph?"

"Yes. It bothers me a little."

"Did you ever know a girl who *wasn't* curious?"

"I never knew many girls."

16

"Then you'll learn. Females have a terrible sense of curiosity. Especially me." She studied my uniform again. "I like the breeches and the black leather puttees."

"I don't. They chafe my legs."

"But if you didn't wear them you wouldn't look so distinctive."

"That's what they keep telling us," I said. "By the way, I drove by the factory yesterday. I didn't see you."

"I was making an entry with Mr. Reece, the office manager. I just couldn't get away. Which way did you come?"

"Through Staleyville, driving south."

"Do you always come that way?"

"Not always, no."

She looked at a tiny wrist watch. "I mustn't keep you, Ralph. See you tomorrow?"

"I'll be parked on your doorstep."

She smiled softly, put the gray convertible in gear, and said good-by. She drove off. I watched the car as it went down the turnpike and disappeared around the bend. There was something exotic about her and I wanted to see her again, to be near her. Yet there was a vague uneasy feeling in me. She *had* asked too many, not-so-innocent questions.

I dressed carefully Sunday. I put on my brown whipcord slacks, brown suède shoes, a green woolen sport shirt and my hound's-tooth sports jacket. I had trouble combing my hair. It was cut so short that no matter how hard I brushed it, it stood up like bristles.

Manette was waiting for me in the living room of the old house on Glen Road. She introduced me to Mr. and Mrs. Fulton Reece, the people she lived with, and she told me Mr. Reece was her office manager at Staley Woolen. Mrs. Reece was quiet, prim and white-haired, with a sickly narrow face and a small, dry-lipped mouth. Mr. Reece was pasty and flabby-faced, quiet and untidy. He was past middle age, but his sparse gray hair was combed crosswise over his skull and seemed artificially waved. He had a remote expression in his eyes. His lips were wet, loose and purplish, and his jaw was slack.

We chitchatted for a moment in the living room. I stood there stiffly and uncomfortably while Mr. and Mrs. Reece sat on the damask-covered divan. The inside of the house surprised me. It had a gracious dignity. There were some oil paintings on the walls and they looked like original old masters. There was no department store furniture, either. Instead, the tables were hand-carved, burnished antiques. There was a deep rich Oriental rug on the floor.

Manette picked up a large wicker picnic basket. I took it from her. We said good-by to the Reeces. They said to have a good time and we went out into the warm bright sunlight.

"What's in the basket?" I asked. "Laundry?"

"Picnic, silly." Manette laughed. "It's such a nice day for one."

"Good stuff," I said. "I haven't been on a picnic since I was a kid. But you shouldn't have gone to all the trouble. I could have had food made up."

"This party's on me. I wanted to show I wasn't a gold digger." She stopped beside the car. "What did you think of the Reeces?"

"I liked Mrs. Reece," I said. "I don't know if I like your boss."

"They're an old Danford family," Manette said, stepping

18

into the car. "Mrs. Reece is a sick woman." Then she looked at me closely. "*Why* didn't you like Mr. Reece?"

"I don't know. Something about his eyes. They weren't normal. Why did you ask? Am I rattling family skeletons?"

Her face flushed suddenly. "They're an old Danford family," she said again. "You should have respect for them."

"Sure," I said. "Sure, I will."

"When Mrs. Reece found out I was alone in Danford, she was kind enough to give me a room here."

"Then that's another reason I like *her*," I said.

We drove out onto the turnpike. She asked me to take Route 105. It was a narrow, secondary road, black macadam, patched and humpbacked. We passed scattered farms, with rocky, hilly fields and gnarled, brown-leafed apple trees. We left the farms behind us and on either side of the road were scrub pines and thick rusty underbrush.

"Where are we going?" I asked her.

"Deer Pond," she said. "Do you know where it is?"

"Yes." I smiled. "But how do you know of it, stranger?"

"A man who works in my office has a cottage on Deer Pond. His name is Cole Boothbay. The office had a picnic there a few weeks ago. It's a lovely spot."

I drove on. There was a narrow, rutted dirt lane. I turned onto it, the car bumping over the potholes, a haze of dust rising behind us. We continued up the road for a mile. There was the crest of a hill and another dirt road to the left, and then we came to a clearing carpeted with brown pine needles. Beyond the trees was the glimmering blue water of Deer Pond. Along the far shore the ridges were flaming with autumn color.

"The yellow cottage," she said. "I borrowed a key in case we want to use the stove."

I drove the car across the clearing, pulled up and parked. The cottage had yellow shingles and green window shades. The shades were drawn. I took the picnic basket and followed her up the three short steps which led to the screened porch. The porch had a gray linoleum, a glider, two plastic-covered chaise longues, a table and four tubular chrome chairs.

She unlocked the front door and pushed it back. Inside it was dark, dank and musty. She opened windows and the pine-scented breeze wafted in. The walls of the living room were pine-paneled, the partitions going as high as the eaves. There was a smoky stone fireplace, battered maple furniture, an old tapestry-covered couch with lumpy cretonne pillows.

"We won't stay in here," she said quickly. "We can bring the lounge chairs down to the edge of the lake."

The water lapped gently along the soft sandy shore. I pushed the empty picnic basket aside and settled into the low-slung chair. She looked at the empty basket.

"Don't they feed you at the barracks?" she asked.

"The food was very good. And I was hungry." I leaned back in the chair, looked up through the pines and saw the deep blue sky and the white cotton balls of clouds. "This is the life," I said. "This is really living."

She laughed and dropped down in the pine needles beside my chair, her black slacks taut over her rounded hips. Her hands reached out and drew my head toward hers. She kissed me. Her lips were soft and fragrant and clinging. She let go. I reached for her again. But there was a trill of laughter from her. She wriggled away and sat down cross-legged on the ground.

"Tell me about yourself," she said.

I grinned at her. "You're smart. Any time you want to stop a man, let him talk about himself. He'll forget everything."

So I told her. I told her I was born and brought up in Cambridge, Massachusetts, not far from Harvard. That I graduated from Cambridge High and Latin and spent a year at Boston University, majoring in chemistry. And how I went into the Army and spent a year in Korea with the Second Division. And how I came home, took the examinations for the State Police, and went to the Training School at Framingham for three months. And, finally, how I was assigned to Troop E.

"And you're going to make it your career?" she asked.

"I once wanted to be a chemist," I said. "Sometimes you never do the things you start out to do."

"Why not?" she asked. "What stopped you?"

"It's a long story," I said. "I'll tell you some time." I turned on my side and faced her. I noticed for the first time the small white scar behind her ear. "Where did you get the scar?"

"When I was a child," she said. "Mastoid. That's why I wear my hair so long."

"It hardly shows," I said. "I'll bet you were the prettiest child in Cleveland."

She looked at me blankly. "Cleveland?"

"Isn't that where you're from?"

"Well—around there," she said, looking away.

"Where are your folks?"

"They're dead. They died when I was very young."

21

"What made you decide to come to Danford?"

She threw a small stone into the lake, making circular, ever-widening ripples on the still water. "Staley Woolen was advertising for clerical help. I'd never been to New England before."

"Do you like Massachusetts?"

"Oh, yes. This part of the state is so rocky and hilly. And the towns with their village greens and white churches are so quaint and historical. There seems to be a certain everlasting strength."

"But you have no friends here. None at all?"

"It takes me a long time to choose friends." Then she smiled at me. "You're the exception to the rule, Ralph."

I reached out and tried to draw her in to me. Her back arched. "Wait, darling," she said. "I have to know something first." Then the words rushed out, tumbling over one another. "Do you believe a girl could meet a boy and in a few days be so in love with him that she'd marry him in a minute? I mean if the boy would have her?"

There was no sound for a moment but the lapping of the water. "Meaning you?" I asked slowly.

"Meaning us," she said tremulously.

"I don't know," I said. "It's been so quick. Sure, I believe those things happen, but—" I stopped. I wasn't sure what more to say.

She turned away from me, her face flushed. She stood up and began brushing the pine needles from her slacks. "I think we'd better go," she said distantly. "The sun is going down and it's getting cool." She bent down and opened her big leather handbag. She took out a metal lipstick tube.

I stood up. "Wait," I said. "I'm sorry. Maybe I was a little abrupt, but you took me by such surprise—" My voice

22

caught in my throat. I had been looking at the handbag and I had seen something gleam inside. "Hold it open," I said.

"What?" she asked. She quickly snapped the bag shut. I took it from her. I opened it again.

I brought out a pearl-handled .32-20 Colt revolver with an ice-blue two-inch barrel. I stared at her.

"It's mine," she said, her face contorted. "There was a pair of them once. I only have this one now."

I broke it open. There were six cartridges in the cylinder. I said, "It's loaded full. You mean you carry this around with you all the time?"

"It's mine." Her lower lip began to quiver. "I own it."

"But what reason could you have for carrying a concealed weapon?" I asked. "What are you afraid of, Manette?"

"Because I've been involved in things," she said in a tight, strangled voice. "You've seen a scar behind my ear. It shows because it's on the outside. But things happened to me inside. Mental things, causing mental scars. They don't show. That's why you think you can keep them hidden."

"What things are you talking about?" I asked harshly.

"Not nice things," she said tonelessly. "Nothing we can talk about."

"We have to talk about it. You're carrying a loaded gun. You don't have a license for it, do you?"

Her laugh was hard, brittle and despairing. "And it's against the law and you're a cop. Where do we go now? To the barracks?"

"Don't be silly," I said. I put the gun back in her bag

23

and handed it to her. "Take it home and bury it in a bottom drawer. Promise?"

"Yes, I promise."

"Now, be a good kid and tell me what the trouble is."

She shook her head. "There's no more trouble," she said in a strained voice. "Nothing is going to happen."

"No, you're in a jam."

"Not now. It's over. I'm going to forget you, Ralph. You can go back to the nice little girl next door. She's for you. Not me."

"How did you know there was a girl next door?"

"Because every boy has a girl next door, or in the next block, or somewhere in his neighborhood. He wouldn't be normal otherwise. And you're very normal, Ralph."

"We're not talking about me," I said. "Don't twist it around."

"I'm giving you your chance to get out. Take it. You don't know how lucky you are. Go back to your girl." Her eyes were brimming. "What's her name?"

"Her name is Ellen," I said. "Look, maybe I don't want to be rushed into things, and I can change my mind about going back, too."

"No, it wouldn't work with us," she said dully. "I thought there was a chance, but there isn't. I shouldn't have bothered to try. Now take me home, please."

I tried to talk to her some more. But she wouldn't listen and she wouldn't answer. Her lips were compressed stubbornly as she began to gather her things.

So I drove her home. She sat silently beside me, her shoulders slumped, her face pale and drawn. When we turned into Glen Road it had grown dark. I walked with her by the lantern post to the front door. She turned to me.

24

"Just one thing more," she said softly. "Would you kiss me good-by, please?"

I put the basket down and drew her in close. Her face came up and I saw her eyes were wet with tears. Then suddenly there was a sharp intake of her breath and her body tensed and her hands gripped my arms. Behind me I heard a car start up. I turned around. It was a black sedan. It flashed by us, went swiftly up Glen Road, its red rear lights dipping over the crest of the hill and disappearing.

"Who was that?" I asked her.

She shook her head dumbly.

"Somebody you know," I said. "Somebody you're afraid of. That's why you asked if I carried a gun. That's why *you* carry a gun."

"No, no," she said. "It's nothing. The noise of the car starting scared me. Probably one of the neighbors."

"Out here in the woods you don't have neighbors. It was somebody sitting in a parked car. What's happening, Manette?"

"I don't know," she said hysterically. "I don't know." Then she wrenched away from me, opened the door and ran inside. The door slammed.

I pressed the bell button. I waited. She didn't open the door. I rang again, picked up the wicker basket. "Tell me," I shouted through the door. I rattled the knob. I waited five minutes. I watched for the light in her room. It didn't go on.

I put the basket down near the door. I went back to my car, got in and drove slowly back to the barracks.

CHAPTER 3 _____

I was getting ready for breakfast Monday morning when Sergeant Ray Beaupré poked his head into my room. "Ralph," he said, "the skipper wants to see you before you go to chow."

Phil Kerrigan was knotting his black service tie in front of the mirror. He turned around to me. "What have you done wrong now, kid?"

"I don't know," I said. I had always been a little afraid of the troop commander. He was a stickler on uniforms, for one thing. I made sure mine was meticulous and correct. I examined the German silver collar ornaments and the polish on my black leather puttees and belts. I gave an extra rub to my whistle, whistle chain and handcuff key and made sure they were shiny.

"How do I look?" I asked Kerrigan.

"Gorgeous," Kerrigan said sardonically. "But if the skipper is going to chew you out, it won't make no difference how pretty you look."

I went downstairs to the troop commander's office. Captain Fred Walsh was sitting behind his desk, his short, muscular trunk tightly encased in the uniform blouse, the captain's bars glinting on the darker blue of the shoulder straps. He looked up and saw me standing there. His heavy eyebrows knitted together for a moment. His mouth was tight, thin-lipped, and his tanned face was creased at the chin.

"Where were you yesterday, Ralph?" he asked.

"At Deer Pond, sir. I was out with a girl."

"All day?"

"Yes, sir."

"Weren't you supposed to go home and see your folks?"

"I guess I was."

"If you couldn't make it, why the hell didn't you phone them?"

"I'm sorry, sir. I should have."

"And last Wednesday, on your night pass, you didn't go home, either."

"Well, I met this girl, sir—"

"Your father phoned me," Walsh snapped. "I don't want your old man calling me and asking if I've got you on punishment duty so you can't come home. And if you're running around with some cookie I'm not going to lie to your old man, either. I've always had a heap of respect for him. He was a damn good, seasoned trooper. Not like what we have now—a bunch of young kids still wet behind the ears."

He looked up at me with his hard, wise, cynical eyes. His hair was wiry with flecks of gray showing around the temples. His neck was thick and ridged with muscles, and

27

his voice had a metallic bitterness to it. He was all cop and nothing else.

"Well?" he asked me. "When are you going to call your old man?"

"I'll call him now, sir."

"Go ahead. And you'll switch nights off with Kerrigan this week. That means you're off Wednesday night again. You go straight home and see your father. Lord knows he's got little enough now in life. It's the least you owe him. And you should know it without being told."

"Yes, sir," I said.

"Sometimes I wonder if you realize what it means for a man to be locked in a wheel chair."

"I realize it. I live with him, sir."

He bent down to his papers. "All right, Ralph," he said wearily. "Go to chow."

I washed my cruiser down. Then I went on patrol, fretful and irritable. I was going to phone Manette as soon as I returned and finished my reports. But while I was at supper she phoned me instead.

"I tried to forget you," she said. There was a quivery catch in her voice. "I swear I did. Don't you think I lay awake all night, seeing that red, sunburnt, peely-nosed face of yours?"

"I didn't sleep well, either," I said.

"Come and see me tonight," she said. "Now."

"I want to but I can't. I'm going on night patrol with Phil Kerrigan."

"When will I see you?"

"I'm off Wednesday night, but I have to go into Cambridge. I have a sick father, Manette."

28

"*When,* Ralph?"

"Next week. Monday. I don't get a day off until then. Why can't you tell me over the phone—?"

"If we had the chance," she interrupted, "if you were willing. Would you take me away from here? Away from this evil city and its evil people—all its filth and badness?"

"Where?" I asked. "Cities are people, not names. You'll find people the same all over."

"I want you to take me away," she said. "Anywhere. To New York, where people can submerge themselves."

"I can't leave the troop," I said. "This is my life now."

"But you could become a city policeman somewhere. You'd have regular hours. You wouldn't have to live in a barracks."

"But I'm a trooper," I said. "It's a lot different from being a city cop."

I heard the breath go out of her. "Forget it," she said. Her voice sounded tired and defeated. "It was a crazy, frantic idea, anyhow. I kept saying to myself, I shouldn't call you."

"You don't have to run away," I said. "There's no trouble that can't be straightened out. If you won't tell me over the phone, we can talk about it when I see you next week."

"I think it will be too late then," she said. "Good-by, Ralph."

"No, wait," I said. "I'll see you when I come back Thursday. I'll try to get away for an hour—"

"Too late, darling," she said softly. She hung up. I stood there with the receiver in my hand. Phil Kerrigan came into the guardroom, taking a last drag on his cigarette.

"Come on, boot," he said. "It's a long night patrol."

29

I put the receiver on the hook. "I don't understand her, Phil."

"Girl trouble, huh?" Kerrigan said cheerfully. "Mostly, it's the hours that spoil it for you. We all go through it."

"No, it's more than that," I said. "And I wish I knew."

My night pass started Wednesday, at 5:00 P.M. I should have left for Cambridge immediately. But at 5:20 I was standing beside my car across from the old house on Glen Road, waiting for Manette Venus.

The Staleyville bus came down over the hill and stopped in front of the house with a swish of its air brakes. Manette Venus stepped out. She was wearing a blue suit, a white blouse, blue shoes and a large blue shoulder bag. Her blond hair was like finespun silk.

She saw me standing beside my car. She ran across the road. I took off my hat.

"What's wrong, Ralph?" she asked, breathing rapidly.

"I was worried about you."

"Oh," she said, looking down at the ground. "Why?"

"Stop it," I said tersely. "Something's wrong. You're in trouble. You can't raise things to a high pitch, then cut them off. You can't leave everything undone, unspoken." Suddenly I reached out and took the shoulder bag.

"The gun isn't there," she said with an awry smile. "I did exactly what you told me. I put it away."

I gave the bag back to her. "I can't go away and leave things unfinished," I said. "If I've done something wrong, if I'm to blame somehow—"

"You made me fall in love with you," she said quietly. "You didn't tell me you had a girl named Ellen. Are you engaged to her?"

30

"Yes," I said.

"Wasn't it wrong, going out with me?" she asked softly. "And making love to me?"

"Yes, it was wrong, and I knew it was wrong, and I made a mistake. But then, you haven't been very frank with me, either."

"So that makes us even," she said bitterly. "It was you who carried things just so far and backed down. What is it, Ralph? Is your conscience starting to bother you?"

"Maybe," I said. "Since I met you I'm all mixed up inside, and that's the truth. It isn't only Ellen. I have an obligation to my family, too. That's where it really starts."

"Now you're bringing your family into it. Why don't you admit your refusal starts with me and nobody else?"

"No, it starts further back," I said. "It starts in 1939 when a man was shot in the back. It seems crazy to go so far back, but that's where it starts."

"You're talking riddles," she said. "I hate riddles."

"It's no riddle," I said. "I'm talking about my father. I'm talking about 1939 when he was a State Police corporal because that's when it begins, that winter when he went out on a call to the town of Lincolnshire. A drunken laborer had been beating his wife and the local, part-time chief of police couldn't handle him alone. My father came there with another trooper to bring the man in. My father took the front of the house. The other trooper went to the back to cut off the rear.

"It was bitter-cold that day. My father came in, turned to calm the hysterical wife and throw the laborer a coat. The man did what was least expected. He reached up over the fireplace, grabbed a rifle there, and shot my father in the back.

31

"The other trooper—his name was Ed Newpole—broke in through the rear door, his revolver in his hand. The laborer turned with his rifle. Newpole shot him through the nose and killed him instantly. But my father's spine was broken and he became completely paralyzed from the waist down."

"I'm sorry," Manette murmured. "I'm terribly sorry."

"Everybody was sorry," I said. "But it didn't help my father. Later, and through the years, the men would come to visit us in Cambridge. Sometimes they'd take my father out to Troop A Headquarters in Framingham, where he'd spend the day. He'd sit at the dinner table in his wheel chair, his pathetic eyes following the sturdy, healthy young men around him. He'd shake his head and say in his day the boys were tougher and had more bounce. Sometimes he'd bring me with him. He'd point to me and say, 'Watch this kid of mine. Wait until he grows up. Then you'll see a *real* trooper.' And as I grew up, they came to see him less and less, they'd invite him hardly ever. It was not their fault. Some of his old friends were transferred far away, the others retired, and the new ones didn't know him. But that was his life, his only life, his only interest. And he couldn't live it himself. And I thought if he couldn't, at least he could live it through me."

Her eyes were thoughtful as I finished. "So there it is," I said. "I grew up and went into the troops. What else could I do? What would anybody else do? You think I could quit and go away, and leave him with nothing?"

"No," she said tonelessly. "And I understand now."

"I wish I could understand *you*," I said. "You've held back, told me nothing. The more you hold back the worse

32

it will get. Bring it out into the open. *Now*, Manette."

She rubbed her forehead so hard the skin turned red under her fingers. "You make it sound so glib and easy," she said. "But there are so many things tangled up in this. Maybe my own life doesn't matter. But there's danger to your own career and your own life."

"Danger to *my* life?" I asked. I took her by the shoulders. I wanted to shake her because she was giving me half-answers again. "What danger? I've been in Danford only three months. I know hardly anybody."

"But people know you," she said listlessly. "They can get to you."

"Now you're the one who's talking riddles," I said angrily. "How can they get to me? And why? And how are *you* involved in it?"

"They're bad people," she said. "I can betray them to you and you can arrest them and lock them up. But I'd have to betray myself, too. And then I'd never see you again."

"But if you turn state's evidence and there are extenuating circumstances—"

"Oh, I'll do it," she said. "I've made up my mind to it. I can't run forever. But first I have to prepare myself. And nobody else can do it for me." Her eyes looked up to mine. "You're going home tonight, Ralph?"

"Yes," I said. "But—"

"When you come back," she said, in a subdued, tired tone, "phone me. I'll be ready with the story then. It won't be a pleasant one, Ralph."

I wanted to argue with her, but there was a stubborn finality in her voice and I knew it was useless to carry it further. "Sure," I said. "As long as you promise."

"I promise. Cross my heart, Ralph. I'll tell you every-thing tomorrow."

And I knew she would. So I left her then. I got into my car and drove away. It was the last time I saw her alive.

CHAPTER 4 _____

WHEN I arrived in Cambridge it was eight o'clock at night. Our house was an old white bungalow with a little white picket fence around it. The lawn was freshly mowed and the leaves had been raked. I knew my mother had been working around the yard. It made me ashamed of myself because I should have been home to do it last Sunday.

I came up the walk to the front porch. The rolled evening paper was there, cast deftly by the bicycle-pedaling newsboy. I picked it up and opened the front door. I caught the savory fragrance of roast beef.

My mother called, "Ralph?"

"Yes, Ma," I said.

She came into the living room. I bent over and kissed her. She was a small, bustling woman, with bright, alert eyes. Her face and her gray hair were damp with the heat of the stove.

"You're almost an hour late," she said.

"I'm sorry, Ma. I was delayed."

"You can't blame us for being worried," she said. "You haven't been home for ten days. I know it's a long trip. But it means so much to your father."

"How is he?"

"The same. He was in his room resting last I knew. He should be up by now."

"I'll go in and help him."

"No. You know how he hates to have you help him into the wheel chair." She stood back and measured me. "You look all famished and tuckered out. Have you lost weight?"

"No. But I'm like a bird dog when I sniff that roast beef. Is it ready?"

"It's been ready for an hour," she said. "Here's your father coming."

He came into the living room in his chrome wheel chair, the one I had bought him with my first two weeks' trooper pay. He was emaciated and gaunt, and his face had a pallor, and his hair seemed grayer than ever before. His hands were blue-veined and bony. He was wearing an open-throated sports shirt. There was my mother's hand-knitted coverlet over his wasted legs. He put his hand out. I took it. I could feel the dry, fragile skin.

"Let's look at this boot trooper," he said with mock sternness. "Push those shoulders back. There, that's better. Ralph, why didn't you come home your last two days off?"

"I got tied up with a few things, Pa."

"It's a long trip, Walter," my mother said to him, quick to defend me. "It's over sixty miles, and after a boy comes off patrol he's tired. I should think you'd speak to Fred Walsh and have Ralph transferred. He could go to Framingham, or Andover, or Concord. Then he'd be much nearer home."

"Now you know that's foolish, Millie," my father said. "They have reasons for stationing a trooper away from his home. It's better he doesn't know any people in his assigned area." Then he turned to me. "How's Fred Walsh?"

"Fine," I said briefly.

"You don't like him, do you?"

"He's tough," I said. "I'll get used to him."

"I worked with Fred quite a few years," my father said. "He's a good cop and a good troop commander. Hard, but fair. Maybe he's a little bitter, Ralph."

"Why should *he* be bitter? He's the troop commander. It's almost like being God."

"Don't be blasphemous," my mother said.

"Fred Walsh has to retire next spring," my father said. "When a man gives his life to an organization—"

"But the younger ones coming up," I said, "they have to have a chance, too. If the older officers stay in grade too long, we'll never make it."

"The young ones," my father said. "Always impatient, restless. But what will a man do when he reaches Walsh's age? He'll be only fifty. Is his life over?" He shook his head sadly. "When I think of it, there ain't many left of the old gang now. Outside of the Commissioner, Major Carradine, Fred Walsh and Bob Clyde in Ballistics, I guess there's nobody left from my time."

"There's Ed Newpole," my mother said.

"Well, I was talking about the uniformed branch. Ed left the troops and went into the detective branch. A detective ain't the same thing." He swung his wheel chair around and faced me. "Anything new in the troops? Any new weapons?"

"There's a new .45 carbine," I said. "It's semi-automatic."

"We never had those kind of weapons," my father said, shaking his head. "When I look back—"

"I think you've bothered the boy enough for now," my mother interrupted. "You go wash up and let Ralph wash up, too."

"Yes, ma'am," my father said, saluting her. He winked at me. Then he wheeled happily out of the living room and bumped the chair over the threshold of the bathroom.

"It's his whole life," my mother said softly. "He talks to me about the troops all day long. And do you see how his face lights up when you come home? You must be kind and patient with him, Ralph."

"Sure, Ma," I said. I patted her cheek and went into the bedroom. I took off my jacket and unstrapped the holstered gun and put it into the bureau drawer. I put the badge in, too. I felt immeasurably lighter now. It wasn't so much the actual weight of the two objects, but the symbols they represented.

I came into the living room with a bath towel in my hand. I picked up the newspaper. I looked across into the dining room and I noticed the gold-embroidered linen tablecloth on the dining room table. Then I saw the folded linen napkins. Instead of the usual heavy tumblers I saw the crystal goblets. There was a silver-plated relish dish and my mother's homemade watermelon pickles. Now she was at the table, moving around, laying out her best silverware. She had changed to a white ruffled apron.

I came into the dining room. "You expecting company?" I asked.

"Didn't your father tell you over the phone?" She

brought her hand up and brushed a stray strand of hair from her eyes. "Ellen Levesque is coming to dinner."

"He didn't tell me," I said, rubbing the stubble on my jaw. "Look, we've known Ellen since she was this high. She's been here to dinner before. You don't have to put out the family heirlooms to impress a kid like Ellen."

"She's not a kid. She's twenty-one."

"Twenty," I corrected. "I'm three years older than she."

"Your father was five years older than I."

"Now what *is* this? Who's talking marriage, Ma?"

"You have," she said calmly. "Often. And with Ellen."

"We never mentioned anything definite. There was no definite time."

"Aren't you in love with Ellen?"

"Sure. Ellen and I—" Then I stopped and I could feel the redness creeping over my face. I was thinking of Manette Venus.

"What?" my mother asked.

"I ought to have time," I said hurriedly. "I'm still in my probationary period and I haven't had my first pay increase yet. I don't think this is the time to talk about it."

"Your father and I have talked about it," my mother said firmly. "We don't exactly blame you for not wanting to come home. It must be dull for you to sit here and talk to a crippled old man, a man who does nothing but relive his life as a trooper. If you had a wife, you wouldn't want to stay in Danford. And your father is afraid you might start hanging around bars and drinking. You know what would happen if you got drunk in a public place. You'd be dismissed from the troops."

"I've never been drunk in my life," I said. "He needn't worry."

39

"But he *does* worry. Well, never mind it now. Dinner was ready an hour ago, and Ellen was waiting for you. She went home for a moment. I do want this to be nice. I've entertained very little since your father's accident. When he was well he liked the little extra touches. You know, I think I'm going to use the silver candleholders."

"Sure," I said. "Why don't you, Ma?"

She put a finger thoughtfully to her mouth. "I think I will. Just this once we'll eat by candlelight. And I don't care if your father does joke that he can't see what he's eating."

"Sure," I said. Then I heard my father come out of the bathroom. I went in to take a quick shower and a shave.

I was putting on a fresh shirt in my bedroom when I heard the front door open. Then I heard my father's dry rasping cough and Ellen's quick, bubbling laughter.

I came into the living room and Ellen whirled around suddenly. She was a china doll of a girl, slim and as supple as a reed, with black wavy hair, green eyes and a saucy, freckled nose. She was wearing a skirt and blouse and her usual flat sandals. She came up and kissed me on the mouth. Then she reached up and rubbed some of her lipstick from the corner of my lip.

"Hello, Ralph," she said. "Your nose is peeling again."

"You know I never could tan." I grinned.

"We've missed you," she said. "We haven't seen you for ages."

"We'll make sure he comes home more often," my father said.

I started to say something, but my mother put her arm around Ellen and said, "Let's go in to dinner."

We had dinner. There was a bouquet of white gardenias

40

Ellen had brought. My father made the expected joke about not being able to see what he was eating and his usual reminiscences about the troops. After it was over, and my father had gone to his bedroom to catch his favorite TV crime program, Ellen and I helped my mother with the dishes. Then my mother shooed us out of the house.

We went onto the porch. Ellen sat down on the porch glider. She took a deep breath. "Indian summer," she said. "The air is hazy and there's a smell of woodsmoke and burning leaves. It's the best time of year. Don't you think so, Ralph?"

"Yes," I said. "Let's ride into Boston and see a show."

"No, let's sit out here for a while."

I leaned against the porch railing and took out my pipe. "Do you mind if I smoke the old incinerator?"

She looked up at me in surprise. "You know I always liked your pipe. You look perfectly handsome in a pipe."

"Thanks," I said, filling it from my pouch. "I have to keep it at home. There's no time in the barracks for a pipe. You go on patrol, go to bed, wake up and go on another patrol. No good for pipe smokers. They need leisure. And you can't sneak a pipe smoke in a cruiser like you can a cigarette."

"You sound a little sullen tonight," she said. "What happened, Ralph? You stayed away from home for ten days. You never did that before."

"Maybe you're just getting to know me."

"After all these years? No, I know you from way back. I remember you from the days when we used to hitchhike to Walden Pond. Or don't you remember?"

"Yes, I do," I said, puffing on my pipe. And I did remember. She had been a gawky little kid then, with thin

41

spindly legs, a skinny boyish body and a tense face. When she ran, the ribbons on her pigtails streamed out in the wind. She had a fierce little temper, erupting like a volcano and subsiding quickly. There was a time when I dropped a frog down the neck of her dress. She raked my face with her nails and kicked my shins, and five minutes later she was all contrite and came running with iodine for my scratches.

"We used to go to Walden Pond," she said. "It was where Thoreau had communed with nature. I often hoped some of the atmosphere would rub off onto us. I used to examine you closely to see if you were turning into a brilliant philosopher."

"It didn't work," I said shortly.

She looked sharply at me. "Nothing seems to be working tonight," she said quietly. "At dinner you hardly spoke a word. It's not like you."

"I didn't get a chance to say a word. My father was telling us about when he was a corporal at Andover. We've heard those stories a hundred times. He keeps looking back all the time. Why doesn't he look ahead?"

"To what?" she asked. "What future is there for him? He's a paraplegic, and inside he's dying by degrees. How much more time does he have, Ralph? One year? Two? Five? Would you deny him the little pleasure of his anecdotes?"

"No, of course not," I said. "I'm sorry. I'm acting like a damn moron tonight. I wish I was like him. I'm not. I don't think I'm cut out to be a cop."

"Why not?"

"Listen, I put in over a hundred duty hours a week. I'd like more time off. At least, I'd like evenings to myself. No wonder they retire a trooper at the age of fifty. He's all beat out by then."

"But you knew all this when you went in." She swung back and forth on the glider. "Ralph," she said gently. "What's her name?"

"Whose name?"

"The girl you met."

I reddened. "What do I have? A glass door in my head? How did you know I met a girl?"

"It shows," she said. "What else could it be? Ralph, what's her name?"

"Manette Venus," I said.

"I see," she said. "You met this girl and that's why you haven't been home. And she doesn't want you to be a trooper, either."

"All right," I said. "So that's what happened."

"Where did you meet this Manette Venus?"

"What difference does it make? I was at a bar having a glass of beer. We started talking."

"You mean she picked you up in a saloon."

"You don't have to make it sound dirty, Ellen. It was mutual. She was lonely. She was a stranger in Danford. She knew nobody."

"So she went to a barroom and picked you up. And never mind the misguided gallantry. You never picked up a girl in your life. You wouldn't know how. And what does she look like? Smooth sultry blonde? Big blue mascaraed eyes and silver lacquered fingernails? Sexy legs and rhinestone high heels on her shoes?"

"She's a blonde, yes. But not—"

"What does she do?" Ellen interrupted. "Work as a hostess in a dance hall?"

43

"No. She's in the office of the Staley Woolen Company."

"But why pick you? What does she want? A good time? Where are you going to get the money to spend on that type? What is she asking for?"

"Nothing. She—"

"You're a big hick," she said, her voice tense and distraught. "She must want *something*. You went after her like a seal after a fish. You swallowed the bait. What happens now? What happens when she spends all your money and gets tired of you?"

"No, you have her wrong. Listen, she's in trouble—"

"You don't owe me any explanation," she said, her face set and rigid. "I'm the little dirty-faced kid next door, remember? I don't have any ring on my finger. We talked about marriage, sure. But what's talk? Talk is cheap. It would be better if I went into a saloon and wiggled a snaky hip at you."

"Look, you're making this sound a lot worse than it is. It's childish—"

"Is it? It's because I thought you were too good for any barroom girl. And it's because I'm a poor sport. And it's because I happen to be in love with a big lug and I don't want to let him go. Now do you want me to open the rest of my diary?"

"No," I said. "Ellen—" I left the railing and went to her. I reached out and tried to take her hands. She slid away and stood up.

"Say good-by to your father and mother for me," she said. "Tell them the flowers and candles were a good idea, but it was a little too late."

"Ellen," I said sharply. "You have it all wrong. I told Manette—"

44

"I could kill Manette," she said. She fled down the stairs and ran across the sidewalk to her house.

I didn't go after her. I knew her, and I knew her temper. It would be a few hours before she simmered down. Until then she would not talk to me. And I knew I couldn't go into the house and face my mother, either.

So I took a walk. I walked down to the Charles River. I walked along the embankment, past the Harvard dormitories and the gilt-knobbed Lars Anderson Bridge. I was in familiar surroundings. I was home. And the more I walked, the more distant Manette Venus became.

I was back in the barracks at 3:00 P.M. the next day, Thursday. I signed in. Stan Maleski was duty sergeant.

"You're back early," Maleski said to me. "You're not due in until four."

"There's somebody I have to phone," I said.

I went into the guardroom and called the Staley Woolen Company office. They told me Manette Venus was out. She had left at noon and had not yet returned.

I called Glen Road and spoke to Mrs. Reece. She said Manette had come home about twelve-thirty and had gone right out again. No, Manette had not explained why she had left work early. But she had told Mrs. Reece to expect her home at six.

At five o'clock I went on patrol with Phil Kerrigan. It had been cloudy, windy and warm all day. At dark it began to rain gustily and fitfully.

There had been a gas station holdup in Connecticut and the two armed men had last been seen heading for the Massachusetts line in a stolen car. We had the cruiser in a roadblock at Route 114. We stood beside it, the intermit-

45

tent rain slashing at our blue raincoats, streaming down our faces, dripping from our cap visors. Kerrigan had his head cocked, watching for headlights in the blackness, listening for tires on a wet road.

I was standing near the open window of the car and I heard the crackle of the shortwave radio. I opened the door and poked my head in. The time was 9:10.

The radio was saying, "—holdup men have been apprehended by Cruiser 19. A Signal Seven for Cruiser 36. Cruiser 36. A Signal Seven."

I called to Kerrigan. "The roadblock's off," I said. "But there's a message for us to call our station."

Kerrigan came over, took off his cap, shook the water from it and got into the car. He radioed the barracks. The dispatcher told us to come in immediately.

Sergeant Ray Beaupré was at the duty desk. I knew it was bad as soon as I saw him. His voice had a tinge of strain in it as he told us Captain Walsh was waiting for me in the troop commander's office.

I went in there, my dripping raincoat making a puddle on the floor. Walsh was in civilian clothes, his necktie hastily knotted and askew, his face darkened by a day-long stubble. He was talking on the telephone and when he saw me he motioned me to sit down. He said, "I'll call you back," and put the phone down quickly. He shuffled some papers on the desk as I took off my raincoat and sat down. He said, "They tell me you know a girl named Manette Venus."

"Yes, sir," I said. "Why? What's wrong?"

"It's bad news," he said.

I waited, my heart beating harder.

46

He rubbed his jaw. "These things a cop sees all the time. He tries to take them in stride. He never expects them to get close to him. I don't know why not. It's the law of averages. A man's got to get hit sometime." He looked at me. "You don't know what I'm talking about, do you?"

"No, sir," I said.

"Manette Venus has been murdered."

"What?" I asked it stupidly, as though I hadn't heard him. "Who?"

"Manette Venus," he said quietly. "She was murdered. Tonight about seven-thirty. The Danford cops notified us over an hour ago."

CHAPTER 5 _____

I was twisting my cap in my hands, pulling at it. Captain Walsh stood up, came around the desk and took the cap away from me.

"Don't ruin a perfectly good cap," he said. He put it on his desk. "The body is at the Danford morgue now. You probably want to see it."

"No," I said, "I don't want to see her."

Walsh stared. "I thought—"

"No, sir," I said. "I knew her when she was alive. I don't want to see her dead, not lying in a long, refrigerated drawer."

"All right," Walsh said. "She's been properly identified by the Reeces. There's no need, I guess." He straightened his necktie. "There's another job we have to do. Do you want a cup of coffee first?"

"No, sir," I said. "What is it you want me to do?"

"You'll come along with me. We're going to see if we can bring in the murderer."

When we left the barracks and got into Captain Walsh's car the rain had stopped and gray clouds scudded across the sky.

"Where are we going, sir?" I asked.

"Out to the Glen Road house where they found the body," Walsh said, starting the car. "How long did you know Manette Venus?"

"About a week, sir."

"Do you know anything about her?"

"She worked at Staley Woolen. And she's originally from Cleveland. Maybe her office can tell us something. They must have an employment record on her."

"The Danford cops are checking there now. There's a record of a former work address in Chicago."

"Cleveland," I said. I had trouble thinking, trouble putting pieces together.

"Chicago, not Cleveland. Her work sheet says she came from Chicago. Why? Did she tell you she came from Cleveland?"

"Yes, sir."

"Hmmm. Do you know if she was in any trouble?"

"Yes, sir, I think she was."

"What was it?"

"She didn't tell me, sir."

"Dammit, son, didn't you ask her?"

"Yes, sir. But she kept stalling me about it. She promised to tell me about it today."

"Well?"

"I couldn't contact her, sir. When I came back from my

49

night pass I couldn't reach her. Then I had to go out on patrol."

"Anything strange about her actions?"

"Yes, sir. She was afraid of something. She used to carry a loaded gun in her handbag."

"What kind of a gun?"

"A .32-20 Colt."

"Did she have a license for it?"

I stared at the road ahead. "No, sir," I finally said.

"And you made no report of it?"

"No, sir."

His mouth was grim. "GHQ isn't going to like it one damn bit."

"I'm sorry, sir."

"You're going to be sorrier than you think. You know why? Because Manette Venus was killed by a bullet from a .32."

Wooden traffic barriers had been put up on Glen Road, blocking off the civilian cars and the curious onlookers. Around the Reece house was a cluster of Danford police cars. The house was ablaze with lights, and spotlights from the police cars were sweeping the rear yard and the woods beyond it.

Captain Walsh stepped out of his sedan and I followed him. There was a group of plain-clothes officers huddled under the lantern post. One of them pushed through and came over to us immediately. He was a short, dapper man with the belligerent air of authority that sometimes a small man has. Walsh introduced him to me as Captain Charles Angsman, Chief of Detectives, Danford Police.

"You find anything yet?" Walsh asked him.

"Nothing new since I spoke to you on the phone, Fred," Angsman said briskly. "The Reeces came home at seven-thirty. As they were getting out of their car they saw this figure run out of the house and head for the woods in back. They went inside and found Manette dead in her room, shot through the head. They called us. We had a squad car here in less than two minutes."

"You think the suspect is still in the woods?"

"I wouldn't know. He was seen running in there. It's a patch of about three or four square miles. I've got it surrounded and cut off. Now we've got to sit and wait for daylight before we can go in. Unless that bloodhound of yours can do something. When is he coming?"

"He should be here any minute," Walsh said. "I called them over an hour and a half ago. He has to be brought from the Andover barracks. In the meantime we ought to keep the back yard cleared so the dog can pick up a scent."

"I did what you told me," Angsman said in a clipped voice. "I've tried to keep my men out of the yard." He stared at me. "Lindsey, what do you know about this Manette Venus?"

"She never told Lindsey anything," Walsh cut in. "He knew her only a week."

"Mrs. Reece said he phoned the girl this afternoon."

"But she wasn't home," I said.

I turned around because I heard a car approaching. It was a pale-blue State Police cruiser with a matching two-wheeled, metal-covered trailer hooked to it. I saw the meshed aperture in the side of the trailer and I knew that Corporal Sam Dutra had arrived from the Andover sub-station with the bloodhound, Nick.

Dutra stepped out and came over to us. He was wearing

a woolen lumberjack coat, rubber knee boots, khaki pants and leather gloves. On his belt were clipped a flashlight and his holstered service revolver.

There was a conference. When it was over Dutra scratched his short sandy hair dubiously.

He said, "What was the weather here?"

"Intermittent rain," Angsman said. "Foggy and warm."

"Any downpours after the suspect ran into the woods?" Dutra asked.

"No downpours," Angsman said.

"That helps," Dutra said. "I don't suppose the killer left anything behind so we can get a scent from it."

"No," Angsman said.

"Well, we'll try," Dutra said. "Let me see the spot where the killer was last seen."

We went into the back yard, crossing the wet springy grass. At the edge of the woods, Captain Angsman stopped. "About here," he said. "This is where the Reeces last saw him."

Dutra asked, "Could they see what he was wearing?"

"No," Angsman said. "All they saw was a shadow run from the house and flit into the woods. It was too dark to see anything."

Dutra went down on his knees, his flashlight moving back and forth along the ground. "There's some bent grass here, Captain," he said. "But it's spread all around."

"Some of my men," Angsman said brusquely. "They were here looking before I stopped them."

Dutra's young face was serious. "Then this here is no good, sir," he said. "I'll have to go farther into the woods."

He pushed into the underbrush. We waited. I could see his flashlight bobbing around in the blackness. He moved to the left in a rustle of leaves. His flashlight stopped bobbing and focused steadily. Then it went off. He came out toward us. His jacket and pants were wet.

He wiped moisture from his face. "There's some broken twigs in there, like somebody went crashing through. I marked it. Now we'll see what the dog can do with it."

Dutra went back to the trailer and opened it. He brought out the bloodhound. The dog whined eagerly. He was a big dog, black and tan, his legs fairly long. He was a purebred hound, yet his tail curled up in peculiar fashion.

Dutra fastened a leather harness to the dog's chest. He uncoiled a twenty-foot strap and hooked it to the harness. Then he picked up the dog in his arms.

He came back into the yard. Walsh handed me a flashlight and said, "You'll go with him, Ralph. Signal us if you find anything."

Dutra went into the woods, carrying the dog. I followed him, snapping on the flashlight. Dutra twisted his head. "I wouldn't use the flashlight, Ralph," he said. "You'll only distract the dog. Your eyes will get used to the dark in a few moments."

I snapped off the light. Now I couldn't see anything. I stumbled into tree branches, scratching my face. Globs of water were dampening my uniform.

I trailed behind Dutra by ear and my eyes became accustomed to the darkness. I saw Dutra put the dog down, but he held the leash taut, keeping the head high. He walked the dog about twenty paces. Then he stopped and peered down. He lifted the dog so that the front legs were off the ground. He held him there for a few minutes. Around me I could hear the dripping of the trees.

Dutra dropped the dog. The dog sniffed, turning his

head from side to side, snuffling close to the ground. Dutra stroked the dog's long ears. He crooned, "Come on, Nick. Good boy. Find him, boy."

The dog strained at the leash and trotted deeper into the woods. Dutra twisted the strap around his wrist and followed him. He called back to me over his shoulder. "I think he's picked up something."

I took my gun from its flap holster and fell in close behind. The trail was tortuous and slippery. I tripped and stumbled over rocks. Ahead of me I saw that Dutra now had his gun by his side.

The woods thickened. In the eerie half-light, fantastic shadows loomed up at me. I heard branches crackle and the wind moaned through the trees. The dog moved with intent certainty through the scrub pines and underbrush, his head close to the ground. The trail twisted. Once the dog stopped, circled and came back again. There was a dull ache in my side. I felt my legs tiring. The big revolver grew heavy in my hand. The bottom edges of my puttees were cutting into my heel tendons and my breeches were now soaking wet. My mouth was parched and my breathing was labored. Dutra didn't falter. His sturdy back moved steadily ahead of me.

The trail grew more erratic and the dog circled more. Whenever he stopped, Dutra would talk to him encouragingly.

We came to a small glade in the woods. It was dotted with broken trees and stumps. At the far edge of it was a small ramshackle hut with a single window and a hanging, gaping door. The dog whined. Suddenly he increased his speed and started straight for it.

Dutra pulled on the leash and stopped him. The dog

54

turned on his haunches and whined again, softly and reproachfully.

I came up. Dutra adjusted the gun in his hand. "The killer may be in there," he said quietly.

"Cover me," I said, breathing heavily. "I'll find out."

"No, wait here. It's my job—" Dutra started to say.

"This one happens to be on me," I said. I ran forward along the edge of the glade, my gun cocked.

"Ralph," he called hoarsely.

I didn't answer him. I moved from tree to tree. I ran across the open space to the side of the hut.

I flattened against it and looked in the tiny window. There was no pane. In a shadowed corner of the hut I saw a darker shadow. The shadow took image—a huddled figure on the floor. I saw a pale arm dangling out, a revolver clutched in the fist.

I waved to Dutra to come on. I saw him dash across the clearing, the dog leaping with great strides ahead of him.

I ran for the door and broke in. A startled white face rose in the corner and screamed shrilly. I dove for it, my hand going for the revolver, knocking it out and away. I heard Dutra's footsteps outside. Then there were three sharp revolver shots as Dutra signaled the others.

The figure screamed again as I bore in and pinned it down to the floor. But something was wrong. It yielded too easily. I was conscious of a soft, slender body against mine. A scent of perfume.

I reached out and pulled the head up. I looked at the shocked, glazed eyes, the freckled nose and the black, lustrous hair. The blood pounded fiercely in my temples, and I closed my eyes and opened them again.

The face hadn't changed. It was Ellen Levesque.

CHAPTER 6 _____

SHE was slumped against the wall, head lolling, eyes dull and unseeing under the beam of the flashlight. She was in a state of shock and she couldn't make out who I was. When I spoke to her she clutched at me and said, "I didn't mean to kill her. I didn't mean to kill her." She kept saying it over and over again.

Dutra picked up the revolver and put it in his pocket. He patted the dog absently. "I never figured it would be a girl," he said in a puzzled voice. "You've been talking to her like you know her, Ralph."

"Yes, I know her," I said bitterly. "I know her well."

"Oh," Dutra said uncomfortably. In embarrassment, he rubbed the big red welts on his hands. He took the gun from his pocket and examined it with his flashlight. It had a two-inch barrel and a pearl handle and I knew immediately where it had come from.

I lifted Ellen in my arms. I went by the dog, sitting

quietly by the door, his tongue out, panting. I carried Ellen out of the shack and started across the glade. I met the other men hurrying toward us.

They took her to Danford Police Headquarters, to the women's detention ward. They made me wait outside the room. I paced the cold floor. A Danford detective leaned against the wall, chewing a toothpick, eying me stolidly.

Captain Walsh came out, his face hard and rigid. I went to him. "How is she?" I asked.

"She's snapped out of it," he said in a cold, flat voice. "She's made a confession. They're going to book her for murder. No bail, of course."

"I have to see her, sir," I said.

"Why? Isn't it enough of a goddam mess?"

"I have to see her," I said tonelessly.

He looked at me for a moment, his mouth pinched. "All right, come on."

We went down the corridor. There was a steel mesh door and a pale, middle-aged woman in a blue uniform coat and skirt. She opened the door. We were in a bare, gray-walled room. There was a long oak table and six hard oak chairs. There were a half-dozen men standing in a corner of the room, one of them Captain Angsman.

Ellen was sitting at the table alone. When she saw me she jumped up and ran to me. Her arms went around my neck. "Ralph," she said simply. She buried her little freckled nose in my uniform.

I looked around at the impassive faces.

"Please," I said to them. "Leave me alone with her. Give me a few minutes."

Feet scraped uncomfortably. I could hear Captain

57

Walsh talking to them in a low voice. He came over to me and said, "They'll give you five minutes. And the matron will have to stay at the door."

We sat at the plain wooden table. The matron leaned against the door, her arms folded in front of her.

"A cigarette?" I asked Ellen.

She took the cigarette. As she bent forward for a light I saw the bedraggled skirt and the muddy coat. There was a smear of dried blood on the collar.

"You hurt?" I asked. "Did they hurt you in any way?"

"Not them," she said. "I'm all right now." She breathed the smoke deeply.

I swallowed hard. "To come into that shack in the woods and find you—" I swallowed again. "I mean, sixty miles from home, in a patch of woods in Danford with a gun in your hand, a suspect in a murder. Everything happening fast like this, all at once. You'd think I was having an opium dream."

"It was horrible," she said. "Horrible. Manette Venus is dead, and I killed her. It makes a tragic triangle, doesn't it?"

"But how could it happen? How did you get there?"

"I wish I had my lipstick," she said distractedly. "They took my bag away. All I have is a receipt. You'd think they'd leave me my lipstick."

I wanted to put my hands on something, to break something. "I don't give a damn about your lipstick," I said hoarsely. "Listen to me, Ellen. This is serious. What *happened?*"

"I know it's serious," she said tonelessly. "The truth is

I'm scared, Ralph. Really scared. Acting this way is a little bit like hysteria—"

"You'd better tell me quick. They've given us only five minutes together."

"I came to Danford to see her," Ellen said.

"Who?"

"Manette Venus. No, not on my own. After last night when we talked, I knew it was all over between us."

"But it wasn't," I said. "You never gave me a chance to explain—"

"Let me finish," she interrupted. "A girl wants to marry a man with a certain strength of character. If he takes up with a barroom hussy, if he's attracted to that type, even if it's just an interlude, it could happen again and again. Worse still, it could continue after we were married. If it's in you to stray, to seek that type of entertainment, it doesn't make for a rosy future, especially when you plan to have children. No, I couldn't marry a man who's away from home all week, and have to worry who his new conquest is —and what new blonde is going to strike his fancy."

"But you've blown this up too big," I said. "You have it all wrong."

"Everything is wrong now," she said. "But I didn't come to Danford on my own. I was talking to your father today, after you left. Your folks knew you were acting strangely and they started to question me. It came out about Manette, about your thinking of leaving the troops, everything. Your father was terribly upset. He said it was an infatuation, nothing more. And if you were so confused you couldn't think for yourself, we had to stop you. He knew you belonged in the State Police, and anyplace else you'd be like a fish out of water. Then he said he had to go to Manette

59

Venus and explain it to her. He asked me to take him to the train in his wheel chair. He's not well at all, Ralph, and, of course, we couldn't let him go. And the only way to stop him was to go myself."

She drew on the cigarette. Her hand trembled, shaking the ash from the tip. "So I called Staley Woolen and got Manette Venus' home address. I took the train to Danford. I got to the station at seven tonight. It was raining and very windy. I took a cab to Glen Road. It was dark and lonely out there. The house was in the woods. I told the driver not to wait because I didn't know how long I'd be."

There was a scrape of feet as the matron at the door changed her position and looked at the big wall clock. Ellen went on hurriedly. "I rang the front bell. There was no answer. There were lights on in the house, but the wind was howling so, I thought nobody could hear the ring. I called out. Then I tried the door. It was unlocked. I went in. There was nobody downstairs. Then I heard a man talking on a radio upstairs. I went up. There was a light coming from under the door of a room. I knocked at it. The radio went off and a girl's voice asked, 'Who is it?'

"I told her it was Ellen Levesque, a friend of Ralph Lindsey's. She opened the door after a moment. It was cold in the room. The window was open and the curtain was whipping around. The rain had come in because the floor was wet. Manette was wearing a quilted housecoat. I expected her to be pretty and she was. I expected her to be nervous, too, and she was. We stood there sizing each other up like a couple of alley cats. She asked me what I wanted and I started to tell her. She wouldn't listen. She asked me frantically to leave. I told her I wouldn't go until I talked. I wasn't traveling a hundred and twenty miles to be kicked out before I had my say. She started to sob and ran for the dresser. She opened a drawer and took out a pearl-handled revolver. She pointed it at me and screamed for me to get out.

"I was mad as anything. I did a silly thing, probably. I made a grab for the gun. I got it away from her and we started to fight over it. The gun went off. Just then I slipped on the wet floor. The next thing I knew there was a flash of lights in my head and I lost consciousness."

The matron came over. "It's way over five minutes, trooper," she said to me. "The girl hasn't been processed yet."

"A few minutes more," I said. "She's only a kid and she's a long way from home."

"Well," the matron said uncertainly. "I'll give you another couple of minutes." She went back to the door.

"I woke up," Ellen said, "with the revolver still in my hand. There was a bump and a cut on the back of my head. Manette Venus was lying on the floor. There was blood all over her face and she was dead. I got up and went to the window. I was dizzy and my head was hurting. Outside, I heard a car drive up to the house and stop. I got so scared and panic-stricken that I ran. I ran down the stairs and out of the house. I didn't know where I was. I kept running, that's all. Then I found myself in an empty shack somewhere and the gun was still in my hand. You know the rest, Ralph."

"When they brought you here," I asked, "did they threaten you or anything?"

"No. Just questions over and over again."

"Did you admit firing the gun?"

"Yes, I did." She looked at me. "But there was something

strange about it. After the gun went off, we kept struggling."

"For how long?"

"At least a few seconds. I don't understand—"

I shook my head. "People have reflexes, Ellen. Even after they're shot they don't usually drop in that split-second."

She rubbed her eyes. "It was so confusing. I wish I could really remember what happened. Anyway, I swear it was an accident. I wouldn't want to harm her. I would do anything to rectify—"

"I know," I said softly. "We'll see what we can do."

"But now," she said urgently. "I mean *now*. I can't stay here—"

The matron came over then and tapped Ellen's arm. "Sorry, dearie," she said. "I'm going to catch it as it is. Time's up, and we've got things to do. Maybe you can talk to him again tomorrow."

"Listen," I said to Ellen. "I'll do all I can. Anything—"

"Why?" she asked in a muted voice. "Because I killed your girl friend?" She stood up and moved listlessly to the door. "Just do one thing. At least, call my father and mother. Please."

"The minute I get to a phone," I said. "And I'll be back as soon as they let me."

Outside in the corridor Captain Walsh was waiting for me.

"We can't let her stay here, sir," I said. "Why, Ellen's only a kid, a scared kid. She just can't stay here, sir."

"There's nothing we can do right now," Walsh said. "You can't interfere with the Danford cops. You've got to let

62

them complete their own investigation. We'll come into it when Boston tells us and not before."

I went into the telephone booth and called Cambridge. When I came out, Mrs. Levesque's shrill sobbing was still ringing in my ears. Captain Walsh was impatiently walking the floor, his hands thrust deep into his raincoat pockets. We went silently down the stairs.

We went outside, into the night air and away from the sour smell of the jail. Walsh said, "You drive. It'll give you something to do."

I drove the cruiser back to the barracks. Walsh sat beside me smoking his cigar. When we reached the blue neon *State Police* sign and turned into the driveway, he coughed brusquely and said, "Take the rest of the night off, Ralph. Go home. Your father will want to see you."

"Thanks," I said shortly.

"The Levesques coming out?"

"They're on their way."

"It's always tougher on the parents," Walsh said. He stepped out of the car. "You get away from the barracks as soon as you can. The newspaper men will be around here like flies around garbage. I can see the headlines tomorrow morning. *Girl Kills Rival Over Love Of State Trooper.* You've made a lousy mess for us, son."

With that he went inside. I watched him, a flush creeping over my face. He had never shown a shred of emotion in the entire time I had known him. And I never hated him the way I did now.

I went upstairs and changed into civilian clothes. When I came down again reporters were milling around in the corridor outside the guardroom. But they were busy watching two Connecticut state troopers in their Stetson hats.

63

The troopers were questioning the two manacled holdup men who had been brought in by Cruiser 19.

In the flurry of excitement I went out the back way. It was past midnight. I took my own car from the parking area and drove out to the turnpike.

But I didn't go home to Cambridge. I couldn't face my father, nor the wordless pain in him, nor the silent accusation of responsibility for what had happened.

I drove instinctively, like a homing pigeon, to the place where it had all started, to the beginning, to a small bar on Berkshire Street downtown in Danford.

The place was more crowded than last time. It was noisier, more smoke-filled. The same undersized bartender was on duty. I hunched onto a stool and ordered a bourbon and ginger. The bartender mechanically put the drink in front of me. I stirred it with the plastic swizzle stick and gulped it down. The bartender began to move away.

"Wait a minute," I said to him. "Remember me?"

He looked at me carefully. He shook his head.

"Wednesday night," I said. "A week ago. About six o'clock. I was sitting here drinking beer."

His forehead wrinkled. He shook his head again. "You're not a regular. A lot of strays come in here, mister. Don't get insulted because I don't remember you."

I said, "A girl came in. Blond, pretty, sapphire-blue eyes, gray suit, no hat. She sat there."

His thin, ferret face twitched in thought. I said, "She ordered an Old Fashioned, but she didn't drink it. Remember now?"

He smiled slyly. "Now I do. Then she came over and

64

picked you up. She took you out of here. How did you make
out, pal?"

"Never mind," I said shortly. "Just tell me if she was in
here before."

He bristled now. "How do I know? And who's asking
the questions? What are you, a cop, or something?"

"Yes, a cop."

"Sure." His lip twitched. "What are they doing, robbing
the cradle now? Go away, you make me laugh."

I took out my wallet and showed him the badge. His eyes
moved back and forth as he read the inscription. But the
sneering, disbelieving look stayed on his face. He spread
his hands on the bar.

I put the wallet back. "I asked if she was here before."

"I never seen her."

"Afterwards?" I asked.

"Never saw her again. I wouldn't forget a dish like her."
He was edging away from me.

I called him back. "I'll have another drink. The same
as before."

He brought it to me. I reached for my wallet again to
pay him. He saw the holstered S&W revolver when I unbuttoned my coat. He wet his lips and his fingers trembled.

I gulped down the second drink. I sat there and stared
at the bar mirror and the red scratches on my face. The
liquor made the tip of my nose and my lips numb, but I
wasn't drunk. I was thinking of Ellen Levesque and the
birdhouse she used to have in her back yard. One time
she had found a robin with a broken wing and she had
cried over it and had made a splint for the wing and built
the birdhouse and padded it with straw. When the wing
healed it was crooked and she painstakingly taught the

bird to fly again. And he did, fluttering awkwardly at first, then he flew away and never came back. And no matter how I tried, I couldn't picture her in Manette Venus' room. Not with a pearl-handled revolver in her hand and Manette Venus dead on the floor near her. My brain was fuzzy and the images refused to focus.

Twenty minutes went by and I had no answer. My glass remained empty on the bar. Cigarette butts piled up in the glass ash tray. But the bartender didn't come back to me.

I heard the front door open and a gush of fresh air hit the room and swirled the smoke. Suddenly the sound in the place became muffled and died away. I turned my drooping head, my eyes moving along the floor. I saw black shoes and shiny black puttees. Then flared dark blue breeches with a broad stripe slashing the sides. There was the horizon blue tunic, the black leather service belt and crossbelt, the State Police patch at the shoulder yoke. Then the square-set visored cap, and under it the rigid face of Patrolman Phil Kerrigan. I peered behind him and saw a young trooper named Ravelli, his thumbs through his belt.

"Hello, Phil," I said to Kerrigan. "You're far off your territory."

His face was expressionless. "We got a call at the barracks. They said an armed kid with a scratched face was here impersonating a state trooper. Asking all kinds of questions. You, Ralph?"

I started to laugh. I couldn't stop. I began coughing. "That's good," I said. "Me, impersonating a trooper. Maybe they feel the same way down at the troop, too."

Kerrigan didn't laugh. Ravelli blinked his eyes solemnly.

66

Kerrigan looked around. "They also said you were getting drunk, Ralph—"

"I'm not drunk," I said. "I'm a little numb, but I'm not drunk."

The bartender came, bent over and spoke to Kerrigan. "It's all right, isn't it?" he asked worriedly. "This guy comes in here and he—"

"No, it's all right," Kerrigan said. "Thanks. You did the best thing." He turned to me and his big strong fingers bit into my shoulder. "Let's go, kid."

"Where?"

"Back to the barracks."

"Captain Walsh gave me the night off. Thanks for the interest in me, but—"

"Look," he whispered harshly. "You're drinking in a public place. If the duty sarge finds out, they'll take your badge."

"I'm not drunk. I've had two—"

"You're half-drunk now. Don't make the mess worse than it is. Come on."

"Take your hand away," I said thinly. "I'll go on my own two feet."

"Fine," Kerrigan said. "Walsh has gone home. We'll sneak you by Maleski and sign you in—on your own two feet."

I went with him to the door. A uniformed Danford cop was standing there. He said something to Kerrigan and Kerrigan said, "Thanks. We'll do the same for you some day."

We went outside. A state cruiser was at the curb. Ravelli turned down all the windows and helped me into the back seat. We drove off. Kerrigan twisted his head around. "How do you feel?"

"How do you expect me to feel?" I asked.

"All right, so you had a bad time tonight. Nobody expects you to be a tin god about it. But next time you want to get drunk, go home and do it. Then nobody'll see you."

"I'm not drunk," I said stubbornly.

"You weren't looking too good," Ravelli said quietly. "Now here's what we do. When we get back to the barracks, you'll walk in alone. We'll be right behind you. Don't talk to Maleski. Sign in. We'll be waiting at the stairway and we'll help you to your room."

"You don't have to stick out your neck for a boot," I said. "I don't expect—"

"Get this straight," Kerrigan said tersely. "We're not thinking of you. If your name wasn't Lindsey—if it wasn't for your old man—I'd turn you in right now."

"You never knew my old man—"

"I've heard of him. Now you'll do as Hank Ravelli says. We'll wait for you at the stairs. If you slip on them going up and Maleski runs out to have a look, then you're finished."

I didn't answer. Ravelli picked up the radio handphone, spoke to the dispatcher and told him Cruiser 36 was coming in.

I shivered. "It's cold in here."

"Leave the windows open," Kerrigan said sharply. "And take deep breaths."

We came to the barracks. They waited outside as I went into the duty office. Sergeant Maleski was at the telephone, his face studiously peering at the desk in front of him. I went by and scribbled my name on the sheet. Maleski put

68

down the phone and Kerrigan came swiftly into the office.

Maleski said, "What was the call in Danford, Phil?"

"Nothing," Kerrigan said stolidly. "A guy was showing a toy badge. The bartender was a little nearsighted."

As they were talking I was out of the office and at the foot of the stairs. Ravelli was waiting for me. He took me up to my room and put me to bed.

"Keep your nose clean, kid," he said. He went out. I could hear his footsteps going downstairs. I waited until I heard the cruiser drive away. Then I put my head on the pillow and fell asleep immediately.

CHAPTER 7 _____

I was all right in the morning. No headache. My mouth was parched and my teeth felt coated, but nothing else. I sat up and looked around. Kerrigan was fast asleep in his bed.

I showered, shaved, dressed in my uniform, and came down to breakfast. In the dining room I saw Captain Walsh at his table. A white-coated mess attendant was putting dishes down on it. As he moved away I saw another man sitting there. He was a slightly stooped, gangling man in a rumpled gray flannel suit. He had lank brown hair and a weatherbeaten, craggy face. He was chewing his food very carefully, with a soft, sorrowful expression. I recognized him as Detective-Lieutenant Edward Newpole from State Police General Headquarters in Boston.

Newpole looked up, saw me, and waved his fork. I waved back to him. Then I turned and spoke to a trooper beside me. The trooper answered briefly and curtly and I looked around at the others at the table. All right, I said to myself. So that's the way it is now.

After chow I lit a cigarette and went to the duty board. I looked up my patrol assignment. My name was scratched. Then I heard Captain Walsh call me. I turned around and followed him to his office. Ed Newpole was sitting there. He stood up and put his hand out.

"How's your father, Ralph?" he asked.

"He's well, sir," I said.

"I guess he might be a little sore at me," Newpole said. "I ain't seen him for a couple of months. I been meaning to—but it's always this and that."

"He often talks of you," I said.

"Probably nothing good," Newpole said dolefully. "We worked together in the troops for a long time. Old Walt never forgave me for going on the detectives. He was always a great one for the uniformed branch. Is he still?"

"Yes, sir."

"Anyway, now he's got you in, and I guess that means everything to him. You try and stay with it, boy. He won't ask for more out of life."

Captain Walsh, lighting a cigar, peered down the end of it. He shook the match and said briskly, "You've got a special assignment, Ralph. An investigation with Newpole. The Manette Venus case."

I stood stock-still, not knowing what to do with my hands.

"Go change to civilian clothes," Walsh said. "It's a break for you, Lindsey. You've got a chance to watch Lieutenant Newpole work. Keep your mouth shut unless you're asked, and maybe you'll learn something." He turned to Newpole.

71

"I never approved of using a boot," he said in a clipped voice. "I've got enough experienced men."

"You know this is an exception, Fred," Newpole said gently. "The boy not only knew the deceased. But he also knows the suspect." He nodded to me. "Go ahead and change, Ralph."

I left them and went to my room. When I came down Newpole was no longer in the building. I found him outside in the driveway, standing by a black headquarters sedan with civilian number plates.

"If you don't mind," I said to him, "first, I have to find out about Ellen. Maybe they released her on bail—"

"No," Newpole said.

"I'd like to see her for a minute. It wouldn't take long, Lieutenant—"

"You'll get a chance later. She's all right. She's seen her father and mother and the family lawyer. They say she's a pretty spunky kid."

"She always was," I said. "What can they really do to her, Lieutenant?"

"Well, I spoke to the D. A. He's going to arraign her on a first-degree murder charge this morning."

"That would never stick," I said. "If it was an accident—?"

"It might stick, and it mightn't. Me, I never speculate. You get a jury, and—you know, you can't figure them." He got into the car. I went around and sat in the front seat beside him. He said, "How do you like it here at Troop E?"

"All right, up until last night. Now the boys look right through me, as if I'm not in the room."

"Well, they'll get over it," Newpole said cheerfully. "You know how these youngsters are. Nobody likes to see the troop get a bad name. You get mixed up with two girls, and one kills the other and it gets into the papers—well, it don't look so good, does it?"

"If they want my badge," I said, "they can have it."

"If they want your badge," Newpole said, starting the car, "they'll take it away without asking. You've only got three months in. You don't even rate a court-martial. Don't throw the badge away so quick, son. It was damn tough getting it."

"I thought if I were free, if I could work on this on the outside, I could do more for Ellen."

"You'd do better with a badge in your pocket and authority behind you."

He drove out along the turnpike until he reached a diner. He pulled into the parking area. "It's time for coffee," he said.

"We just had coffee."

"It'll give us a chance to talk. I talk better with a cup of coffee in my hand." He opened the door and stepped out. I started to follow him.

"No," he said. "I'll bring the coffee back here. We'll talk in the car."

He came back with two steaming cardboard coffee containers. I sipped on mine. The coffee was fresh and strong, but there was a wet paper odor from the carton.

Newpole cocked a side glance at me. "I hear you threw a little wingding at a bar last night."

I started to answer him, but he went on. "It gets around. You can't outfox an old hand like Maleski. He's seen every trick in the book. But as long as you didn't rub his nose in it—"

"Also because I'm Walt Lindsey's son," I said bitterly.

73

"Why don't you say it? If it was anybody else who did it—"

"A boot, you mean?" Newpole said amiably. "Sure, he'd be out. I guess nobody wants to stick a knife in your old man. So you got a break. If you're smart, it don't happen again."

"I wasn't drunk," I said. "I only had two."

"I've seen folks get drunk on one. Anyway, let's say you were upset."

"Yes, I was upset. By God, it was Ellen Levesque. They have her in a cell. A kid who would never step on an ant."

He sipped carefully on his coffee, his pale brown eyes roaming the parking area. "I remember her around your house. Cute little black-haired girl? Freckles?"

"All over her nose."

"That's her," Newpole said. "Maybe we'd better start this thing from the beginning—with the other one. How did you meet Manette Venus?"

I told him. I began with the barroom on Berkshire Street. I told him of the gun, of her fear, everything. When I was through he said, "Did you really fall for this Manette?"

"I don't know," I said. "She was a beautiful girl, the kind who would attract any man. I don't know how long it would have lasted or where it would have led. I didn't know her long enough."

"You wouldn't have gone away and married her?"

"I don't think so," I said. "You get all excited about those things in a sudden flash. Then later when you think about them, you're not so sure. Because all the real problems come up and stare you in the face." I twisted around to him. "They sent you down to investigate me, too, didn't they?"

Newpole took a last sip of his coffee and tossed the con-

74

tainer out the window. "Sure, I won't kid you. It's one of the reasons. I'm supposed to take your badge, too, if there's any culpability on your part. That's the word the Commissioner used, culpability."

"And that's why I was assigned to the case. So you can keep an eye on me, watch me, examine me under a magnifying glass."

Newpole scratched the end of his nose. "Can't deny that, either," he said sadly. "But you got to look at it this way, too. It's a small, handpicked organization. It's got a good reputation. The Commissioner is pretty fussy about it. He has to be. A trooper is out alone most of the time. Sometimes twenty, thirty miles away from his base. When a man's alone and far away, he has to carry a lot of authority. You've got to be sure of a man like that. 'Course there's also an obligation to your old man. But if you get panicky and run—if you quit—"

"No, I won't quit," I said. "Not now. They'll have to kick me out."

"Good," Newpole said, pleased. "It's the best thing you've said. I was afraid maybe you'd go soft—"

"If there's any—what did the Commissioner call it?"

"Culpability," Newpole said.

"If there's any culpability," I said, "I'll take it. What did they think I was, Lieutenant?"

"They didn't think anything—yet." He looked at his watch. "Well, I think it's time to go down to the Danford Police and stir things up a bit."

We were standing in the office of the Homicide Squad at Danford Police Headquarters. There was a long, scarred walnut table, and sitting behind it with the Venus file in his hands was Captain Charles Angsman.

"This is what we've got on Manette Venus so far," Angsman said, tapping the folder. "The girl came to Danford a month ago to work in the mill. The Reeces have no children so they rented a spare room to her. We don't know yet where Manette Venus came from originally. There's a work ad from Chicago and that might help. We sent out a GBC for next of kin. It's going to take time to find out." He swung the chair around and looked at me significantly. "Lindsey, you sure you don't know anything about her?"

"I guess she never told Lindsey much," Newpole cut in. "What else, Charlie? What about her employment record at Staley Woolen?"

"Nothing, Ed. She gave her boss, Reece, her social security number, the old work address in Chicago and nothing else. I sent her fingerprints to Washington." Angsman took off his hat and rubbed the nap very carefully. He had glossy black hair. He yawned. "What are you so interested in, Ed? What's *your* pitch?"

"Well," Newpole said, "I was wondering how strong a case you had against Ellen Levesque."

"Strong enough," Angsman said. "We found her with the gun. She admits firing the shot."

"You got a statement from her?"

"Yes. She admitted it in front of witnesses. It'll stand up. I don't care how many friends she has in the S. P., or how many connections, either."

"Nobody said anything about connections," Newpole said coldly. "And nobody asked for a break for her, and nobody's trying to cover anything. And that goes from Boston all the way here."

76

"It's been done before," Angsman said.

"Not with us," Newpole said. "I don't know about the Danford cops."

Angsman's face turned a mottled red. "If you're making any cracks about local cops—" he said furiously.

"Oh, come off it, Charlie," Newpole said amiably. "I like local cops. All my life I've worked with local cops. Without them we'd have to close up shop. But every once in a while we run into snags in Danford. It's one of those kind of towns. And you know it better than I do, Charlie."

"I don't run the Danford P. D. But just the same I'm touchy about it."

Newpole smiled wryly. "Hell, another one of these sensitive cops." He tapped Angsman's shoulder. "I'm sorry if I rubbed your fur the wrong way, Charlie. Come on, I'll buy the coffee. Then we'll all go over to the Reece house."

Angsman's jaw muscles relaxed. "If you wait, I got a phone call to make first."

I sat in a corner of the Reece living room and watched Ed Newpole talk to Mrs. Reece. He was polite and sympathetic. He sounded easy going and careless, yet he slid pointed questions in with such unobtrusiveness that Mrs. Reece was unaware how exacting and thorough he was. Again and again he asked the same questions simply by rephrasing them, as he checked her story for inconsistencies.

When he was through we found out Manette had come home at six last night. The Reeces left five minutes later to attend a dinner of the Danford Pioneers. Because Mrs. Reece wasn't feeling too well, they had come away early and arrived home at seven-thirty. As they stopped the car they saw the front door open and someone run out of the house and disappear into the woods in back. They had run upstairs to see how Manette Venus was. Her door was open. She was lying on the floor of the bedroom, covered with blood. They had closed the door, rushed down and phoned the police. Then Mrs. Reece fainted away from the shock and fright.

Newpole smiled reassuringly at her. "You touched nothing in the bedroom, I'm sure."

"Of course not," Mrs. Reece said, her fingers plucking at the crepelike skin of her throat. "We took one quick glance and ran."

"And you have no description of the person running from the house," Newpole said. "The light was bad?"

"Very poor," Mrs. Reece said. "And we were a distance away."

"Did Manette ever speak to you of her past, Mrs. Reece?"

"No. She was well-bred and exceptionally quiet. Many times I tried to draw her out, but she evaded the subject. We made every attempt."

"She lived with you a month," Newpole said casually. "I bet the whole time she was here something was bothering her."

"Yes," Mrs. Reece said. "Sometimes at night we could hear her crying in her room. But never a word from her. It would break your heart to listen to her. When I spoke of it, she said it was nightmares."

Newpole tugged at his chin. "She was in some kind of trouble," he said, as though to himself. "She never mentioned having enemies, did she?"

"No."

"Who were her friends, Mrs. Reece?"

78

"This young man here. Ralph Lindsey." She turned to me and smiled tiredly. "You were her friend, weren't you, Mr. Lindsey?"

"Yes," I said. "I think I was her friend."

Newpole said, "Did she ever mention a Cole Boothbay?"

"No," Mrs. Reece said. "But there was a girl named Helen Toledo. An older girl."

Newpole asked how it was spelled and he wrote it down in a tattered, dog-eared notebook. He said, "Did Helen Toledo ever come here, Mrs. Reece?"

"Twice. And not Manette's type at all. Helen Toledo was a big redheaded girl. She was a waitress in some saloon. The second time she was here I could smell liquor on her breath. I'm sure Manette didn't drink. She didn't even smoke. And she did love this house so, and all our cherished antiques. I was the one who asked Fulton to board Manette here. Not only because the money was helpful, but also for her companionship." She smiled vaguely and sadly at us. Her eyes were focused somewhere in the distance, going back to a different time, a different era. "The house wasn't always like this," she said softly. "In those days it was a country house, and when Fulton and I first came here it was bright and shiny like a new penny. There was a carriage house and a stableboy and a groom and a coachman. The servant quarters were on the top floor." Her head flicked, her sad eyes fastened on Newpole. "Times change, sir," she said. "Fortunes fall. When they do, one must carry on somehow. One cannot allow circumstance to subvert the morals. We have many debts and we are grateful to the Staleys for providing Fulton with a job. But it is merely a job, a subordinate position, and we don't have nearly the income we formerly had. Do you understand, sir?"

79

"I understand," Newpole murmured gently.

Angsman bent forward in his chair, his nimble, restless fingers smoothing the nap of his hat. He said, "Mrs. Reece, what about Mr. Lindsey here?"

"I met Mr. Lindsey only once," she said. "He impresses me as being a nice young man. Shy and a bit reserved."

"I mean, how did Manette feel about him?" Angsman asked, his voice sharp and metallic. "Did she confide in you?"

"We shouldn't really discuss it in front of Mr. Lindsey, should we? A private matter—?"

"If you want him to leave the room—" Angsman said.

"No," she said. "The girl is dead. It makes no difference now if I reveal a confidence of her heart. As it happens, Manette and I spoke of Mr. Lindsey yesterday noon, when she came home early from the office. I was asking her if she liked him. She said it was more than liking. He was everything she had ever wanted. Then suddenly she burst into tears and fled upstairs. I couldn't understand it." She turned to me, her face grave. "Mr. Lindsey," she said directly. "Didn't you reciprocate her feelings?"

The back of my neck was damp. I could feel redness creeping over my face. "Mrs. Reece, I knew her such a short time. It's hard to—"

"It's not so important now," Newpole broke in. "Mrs. Reece, do you mind if we go upstairs and have a quick look at her room again?"

"You may, Lieutenant. I have her clothes packed away in her suitcase, waiting for someone to call for them. Have you found any of her family yet?"

"Not yet, ma'am," Angsman said.

We left the living room and climbed upstairs. On the

landing, Newpole said, "Charlie, what do you know of the Reeces?"

"They're prominent in town. The husband, Fulton Reece, is from one of the first families in Danford. Pioneer stock."

Newpole took off his battered hat and scratched his head. "The old mansion's been run into the ground," he said.

"They've had a tough time. They owed quite a bit of money around town, but at least they managed to hold onto their antiques. Mrs. Reece is a sick woman and a lot of dough went to hospitals. Finally, the Staley people took Fulton in and gave him a job. These old families will stick together when they can."

"What's wrong with Fulton Reece?" Newpole asked. "He inherited money, didn't he? With his background, you'd think—"

"He might be a little soft," Angsman said stiffly. "Sometimes these old families will turn out a soft one."

Newpole shook his head and frowned. "Let's take a look at the girl's room, Charlie."

We went inside. The first thing that struck me was the scent of roses. I saw them in a green vase beside the small radio on the bedside table. There was a maple spool bed with a white candlewick spread. There was a maple chest of drawers. The maple dressing table had an oval mirror over it, a gay fabric covering the sides and front. There were two maple ladder-back chairs with bright seat covers. On the windows were white crisscross curtains.

"Manette Venus was here on the floor," Angsman said. "She was lying on her back on the gray shag rug. The rug is down to the lab now. We're checking it for blood type." He went across the room and stood in front of the pink, flowered wallpaper. "This is the south wall," he said, point-

ing to a gouged-out bullet hole. "We dug the bullet out
here. The lab men went over the whole room. Not another
mark in the joint."

"What was the caliber of the bullet?" Newpole asked.

"It was a .32-20 slug."

"Copper-jacketed?"

"No, the slug in the wall wasn't. The gun was a pearl-
handled .32-20 Colt with five copper-jacketed cartridges
and an empty shell still in the cylinder. One had been
fired."

Newpole rubbed the side of his jaw. "But you said the
bullet in the wall had no copper jacket."

"No," Angsman said irritably. "That's the one thing I
don't understand yet."

"There was another gun," I said.

Newpole turned around. "What other gun?"

"Manette mentioned she once had a pair of these pearl-
handled revolvers."

"Once," Angsman said acridly. "And how long ago is
'once'? And where is the second one?"

"She didn't tell me," I said. "But it might be important."

"We'll keep it in mind," Newpole said.

"I don't see where it means much to us now," Angsman
said. "There's only one gun and one bullet involved here."

Newpole pushed his battered hat back. He stood with
his hands on his hips and surveyed the room. He went to
the closet door, opened it, and peered inside.

"That closet door," Angsman said, "was slightly ajar. I
figure the girls were wrestling around near it and Ellen
Levesque bumped into it. That's where she got the crack
on her head."

I was at the window. I opened it and looked down at the ground. Newpole came over beside me and pushed the frilly white curtain aside. "I know what you're thinking, Ralph," he said quietly. "But nobody could have come up this way. This is the second floor. The sides of the house are smooth. There's no grip. And no trees around, either."

"There's a garden bed down there," Angsman said. "Anybody walking around outside the window would have left footprints in the soft earth. You can go down and see for yourself."

Newpole came back to the center of the room. "Charlie," he said, "have you had a chance to talk to Helen Toledo?"

"Mrs. Reece mentioned her last night. I sent a man to interview the dame. She claims she knows nothing. She was working last night at the Starlight Café. Been working there for months. I don't say it's the worst joint in town, but it's low enough down the ladder. Manette came in there a month ago. She told Helen she was a stranger in town and didn't know anybody. So Helen saw her a few times. They went to a movie. A restaurant, once or twice."

"Manette never confided in her?"

"Helen says no."

"Listen," I blurted out. "Something's wrong with this whole deal. Manette told me she knew not one solitary person in Danford, outside of the office workers at Staley Woolen. She couldn't have known Helen Toledo for a month. She wouldn't have gone into a dive like the Starlight Café—"

Angsman snorted. "No? You think she was a wide-eyed innocent baby?"

"She was a refined kid," I said.

83

"Then what was she doing with a key to Cole Boothbay's cottage?"

"She borrowed it for the day. There had been an outing there once. If you'd talk to Boothbay—"

"We're way ahead of you," Angsman said. "I sent a man to Staley Woolen the first thing this morning. Boothbay is an accountant there. He knew the girl, all right."

"She worked there," I said. "Naturally she'd know him."

"She knew him well," Angsman said. "*Very* well. And, in the past month, she was at the cottage *more* than once."

"Not alone," I said harshly. "She wouldn't go there alone with him."

"Wouldn't she?"

"What did Boothbay say?"

Angsman laughed mirthlessly. "He says there was always a chaperon, always somebody from the office. What else would you expect him to say?" He straightened his jacket and adjusted his natty hat. "Stick around, boy. You're learning about life."

"Manette lied to you, Ralph," Newpole said gently. "And more than once, too. With some people a lie is the shortest distance between two points. You'll have to learn not to take allegations for truth. You've got to sift and check everything they tell you. It's monotonous drudgery, but I don't know of any short cut."

"But why?" I asked. "What reason would she have for telling me these things?"

"That's what we have to find out," Newpole said, rubbing the side of his nose. "Charlie, who's doing the autopsy on the Venus girl?"

"Dr. Lloyd Dirksen, the medical examiner, and a State

Police pathologist, Dr. Neary. They're at the city morgue with it. They may be finished by now. You want to see them?"

"Very much," Newpole said.

CHAPTER 8 _____

I sniffed the strong odor of disinfectant as I
sat on the hard wooden bench outside the autopsy room.
It was in the basement of the Danford General Hospital and
there was a cold concrete floor. Ed Newpole tapped his
feet against it, humming tunelessly. He took out a pack of
cigarettes and offered them to Captain Angsman and myself. As we were lighting up, Dr. Dirksen came out through
the swinging doors. He was a thin-shouldered man of fifty,
with a hollow-cheeked face and sparse, gray-streaked hair.
He stopped when he saw Captain Angsman.

"Hello, Charlie," he said briskly. "You waiting to see
me?"

"Me and Ed Newpole, Doc."

Dirksen peered down. "I didn't see you, Lieutenant."
He laughed shortly. "This place is like a morgue." He bent
over and gave Newpole a brief, hurried handshake.

Newpole said, "Doctor, this is Ralph Lindsey, one of our troopers."

I stood up. Dirksen's eyes squinted as he poked his hand out to me. "Oh," he said. "So you're Lindsey." He turned abruptly to Captain Angsman. "The Venus case. Right?"

"That's right, Doc," Angsman said. "You finish her yet?"

"All through," Dirksen said. He took a cigarette from Newpole with a quick, nervous gesture and sat down on the bench. "Good Lord, this early in the morning and I'm all fagged out. Dr. Neary already left. There was nothing unusual about the autopsy. What is it you want to know?"

"First, the physical condition of the body," Newpole said.

"She was a healthy young woman," Dr. Dirksen said. "Well-formed, fully matured. Of course, there was a bullet hole through her head. The entrance being about an inch over the left eye. The dispersion of powder residue, Dr. Neary tells me, shows the bullet was fired close, probably not more than six inches away. The remainder of the body was unmarked, unblemished. Well, not exactly. There was a small scar behind the right ear. She had a mastoiditis when she was a child."

"The bullet was supposed to be a .32-20," Newpole said. "The gun found on Ellen Levesque was a .32-20, with five copper-jacketed cartridges. One shot had been fired. Yet the bullet recovered in the room had no copper jacket. Which would lead me to believe that some other—"

"Hold it," Dirksen said. "We found some copper fragments in the girl's body."

"Where, Doctor?"

"In the girl's brain. Maybe Buchanan, the Danford ballistician, can tell you about them. He's in the autopsy room now, finishing up."

Newpole drew slowly on his cigarette and looked at me with the corners of his mouth turned down. I cleared my throat. I said, "Doctor, could I ask you something?"

"Go ahead, Lindsey."

"Would you say that Manette Venus was killed instantly, sir?"

Dr. Dirksen ground his cigarette under his heel. "We think so. Why?"

"This, sir. Ellen Levesque said after the gun went off in her hand she struggled with Manette Venus for several seconds. If she had shot Manette, how could Manette still fight with her?"

A short, cynical laugh came out of Angsman. "What makes you think Ellen is telling the truth?"

I whirled around to him, my fists clenched. "Listen," I said. "I—"

"Now wait a minute," Dirksen said. "It's a logical question. Supposing the girl *was* telling the truth. We've had cases where people have been shot through the brain and haven't died instantly." He turned to Newpole. "Lieutenant, you remember the Delehante case a few years back. You worked on it."

But I remembered that one myself. We had had it in a course at the State Police Training School. The victim had been a domestic named Gertrude Delehante. She had been found dead in the woods outside Danford with a bullet hole in her right temple. She was lying in the underbrush naked and covered with blood. Her clothes were strewn around in an area of twenty-five feet. And thirty feet away was a bloodstained, twenty-two-caliber rifle.

"You remember how we thought that one was a murder," Dr. Dirksen was saying. "But when we reconstructed it, it turned out to be a suicide. We learned Gertrude Delehante had held the rifle to her right temple and yanked at the trigger with her right thumb. The bullet passed through her brain behind her eyes. But she wasn't instantly killed. She was totally blinded and insane and she wandered about naked in the underbrush until she died. Am I right, Lieutenant?"

"That's what happened," Newpole admitted.

"So the Venus murder could be a similar case where death didn't come instantly." Dirksen stood up. "That's all I have to say, gentlemen. I must run along. I have a meeting with the county health officer in ten minutes. Charlie, the assistant D. A., Dennis Hackberry, is still in the autopsy room. When he comes out, will you tell him I've gone? I'll send him the autopsy report."

"Sure, Doc," Angsman said. Dirksen nodded to us, clamped his hat on his head and left. I sat down again and looked at Newpole. His face was noncommittal.

The door to the autopsy rooms opened again and three men came out talking. I recognized the assistant district attorney, Dennis Hackberry. He was a waspish, elderly man with a bony face and red broken veins in his cheeks, white hair and a bent posture. Behind him was a State Police Detective-Lieutenant, Chester Granger of the district attorney's staff. The other man was carrying a black microscope case and I didn't know him.

"Hello, Ed," Lieutenant Granger said. He was chewing gum. He was a tall, loose-jointed man with a prominent jutting nose and a nervous, fidgety manner. "You here, too, Lindsey?"

89

"Yes, sir," I said.

"This is Mr. Hackberry, the assistant D. A.," Granger said to me. "The gentleman with the microscope is Bill Buchanan, the Danford police ballistician."

We shook hands all around. Hackberry stared at me in disapproval, his mouth narrowed. Then he turned to Angsman and said, "Where's Dr. Dirksen?"

"He had an important meeting," Angsman said.

Hackberry looked at his wrist watch. "I've got to beat it. I have the arraignment at the district court."

"What are you going to charge her with?" Newpole asked.

Hackberry turned as though surprised. "Why, murder, Ed. We'll bind her over for the Grand Jury."

"I don't know," Newpole said mildly. "Ellen Levesque claims it was accidental."

Hackberry stared at him. "Oh, she does, huh? Tell him, Chet."

"It's a strong case, Ed," Lieutenant Granger said. "The motive is sound. It's a jealousy affair. Manette had taken Ellen Levesque's boy friend away. So Ellen came down from Cambridge and forced her way into the Reece house—"

"It's not so," I interrupted. "Ellen wasn't jealous."

"Weren't you engaged to her, Ralph?" Granger asked, chewing his gum, his jaws moving like a squirrel's. "And didn't you have a big fight the night before over Manette Venus?"

"Yes. But Ellen was sent to Danford by my father. And she didn't *force* her way into the house. She said the door was unlocked."

"She made illegal entry," Granger said. "You've got to

90

face the fact she was a trespasser. She forced her way into Manette's room. There was a fight. Manette tried to defend herself with her gun. Ellen took it away from her and killed her with it. Then she took off."

I looked helplessly at Newpole. He said, "Well, Ellen didn't bring the gun there. You're going to have trouble proving deliberate malice aforethought."

"How much premeditation would she need?" Hackberry asked. "A day, an hour—a minute? The opportunity presented itself and she used it. But why argue with me, Ed? Let the jury decide if it's a lesser charge. Of course, if she wants to plead second degree I might discuss it with her attorney. It would save the expense of a trial."

"Ellen was struck on the head, sir," I said stubbornly. "She was unconscious for some time."

"Oh, was she?" Hackberry asked. "Let me tell you this, sonny. I know murderers. I've been up against a lot of them and I know all their angles. We had a doctor examine Ellen Levesque. Yes, there was a laceration and a slight concussion on the back of her head, but Ellen herself admits it occurred in the struggle with Manette Venus. She claims she was knocked out. But I'll lay you dollars to doughnuts the girl wasn't knocked out at all. She killed Manette just before the Reeces came home. When she heard them arrive, she made a break for it. She ran over, opened the window and was going to jump. But it was too high. So she ran out of the house with the gun in her hand. Luckily for the Reeces, she got away before they left the car. Otherwise she might have used the gun on them, too."

"That's not evidence, sir," I said. "It's only guesswork."

"Don't tell me what's evidence," Hackberry snapped. "The only evidence I need is that Ellen Levesque admits firing that one shot. She had the motive, and the intent was there. The bullet struck Manette Venus, went through and lodged in the wall. It came from a .32-20 Colt which you yourself found on Ellen Levesque in the woods."

"It's neat and tidy except for one thing," Newpole said. "The gun contained copper-jacketed cartridges. The bullet in the wall had no copper jacket."

"You're not going to harp on that, are you?" Hackberry said. He motioned to Buchanan. "Bill, tell them what you found."

Buchanan nodded his head. "We found fragments of the copper jacket in the girl's brain. Those copper jackets will separate sometimes, especially when the bullet strikes a hard object. Bone in the skull, for example."

"Could you determine the caliber of these fragments?" Newpole asked.

"Yes," Buchanan said. "I examined them under the mike. The same as the bullet. .32-20. They match the bullet perfectly. Then there's the empty cartridge shell in the gun cylinder. The shell matches the bullet, too."

Newpole scratched his nose. He said, "Mr. Hackberry, what if she pleads self-defense?"

"Self-defense?" Hackberry asked. "Are you crazy, man? How can she say self-defense when she barged into that house? How can she claim *she* was attacked. The jury would laugh at her."

"Then there's only one more thing," Newpole said. "I'd appreciate it if Lieutenant Granger would collect all the material evidence in the case. I'd like him to show it to GHQ."

"What for?" Hackberry demanded.

92

"GHQ would like to have a look," Newpole said gently. "Routine, more or less. You don't mind, do you?"

"No," Hackberry snapped. "That's Lieutenant Granger's department. But you'll have to wait a few days until I'm ready to release it." He flung his cigarette across the room. It hit the concrete floor in a shower of sparks. He left us without another word. As I watched him go, there was a sickening, hopeless feeling in me.

Angsman pursed his mouth in a soundless whistle. "You hurt Hackberry's feelings, Ed. D. A.'s don't like to have their judgment questioned by cops."

"There's always a first time for everybody," Newpole said calmly. "They've questioned *my* judgment plenty of times. Charlie, would you mind if Bill Buchanan brought those copper fragments into Boston?"

"Hell, I don't mind," Angsman said sardonically. "Do you, Bill?"

"No," Buchanan said stolidly. "I don't mind at all. I always like another opinion."

"Fine," Newpole said. He set his hat on his head and motioned to me. "I've got a few things to do, Ralph. So I won't need you for a while. I'll have Chet Granger drive you back to the barracks."

I nodded my head mutely. I knew what it was. He was going to appear at the arraignment of Ellen Levesque for first-degree murder. And he did not want me to see her there, a frightened, bewildered girl locked in the prisoner's cage as though she were some wild animal.

CHAPTER 9 _____

IT wasn't until I had put on my uniform again and had reported for duty that I realized it was almost Friday noon. I took a cruiser from the garage and went out on my Staleyville patrol. I used the alternate route on 129, nearing the Staley Woolen Company from the south with the sun at my back. I stopped and waited until I saw the armored pay truck pull away from the factory gate and head down the road toward the center of Staleyville.

I started the car and drove up slowly. When I reached the gate, I picked up the handphone and called into Troop E. I gave them a Signal Eleven on Cruiser 36 that I was going off the air at Staley Woolen Company.

I brought the car in through the gate, past the startled old guard in his gray uniform, and stopped at the two-story, red-brick office building. The riveted steel front door was locked. I rang the bell. A slit in the steel door opened and a guard showed his eyes. He unlocked the door. I asked for the office manager and was told he was upstairs.

Mr. Fulton Reece's office was a small, glass-partitioned cubicle. His desk was cluttered with papers. His face was unusually red and perspiring. His suit was untidy, his shirt collar soiled. His eyes were abnormal, pupils enlarged, the movement constantly shifting.

"I'm very much upset about Manette Venus," he was saying. "I was looking at her employment record a little while ago. It's surprising how little we knew of her, poor child."

"Could I see the employment record, sir?"

"Of course. Sit down, won't you?" He fumbled around the desk, moving a tangle of papers. Then he pushed down a lever on his sound box. He spoke into it. He snapped off the lever and looked up at me. "They'll send her folder right up."

I sat down in a brown leather chair. I said, "Do you have a Cole Boothbay working here?"

"Yes," Reece said. "He's been with us over a year. Very good man. Efficient, industrious and the type who simply radiates self-confidence. I rely upon him a great deal."

"Do you know anything of his personal life, sir?"

"Nothing." His round full mouth pouted. "You'd hardly expect me to poke my nose into—"

"I thought perhaps Mr. Boothbay might have told you things."

"Hardly. There'd be no occasion."

"And that goes for Manette Venus, too?"

"Naturally. Neither my wife nor I knew anything of her personal life."

It was going badly and I did not know what to ask next.

95

A fluffy-haired girl came into the office, carrying a Manila folder in her hand. She moved by me in a flurry of lilac scent and handed the folder to Reece. She went out. I could see her walking along the counter that ran the length of the main office. She leaned over and spoke to a girl sitting at a typewriter. The girl looked at me and giggled. Another girl left her desk and the three of them whispered together.

Mr. Reece watched them with harried eyes. He stood up uncertainly, then sat down again. "You're disrupting the office, Mr. Lindsey. I imagine the uniform is creating quite a stir with the girls." He opened Manette Venus' folder and turned it around to me.

There were two pages. I read them rapidly. "It's not much, Mr. Reece."

"I told you it wasn't."

"She gives a reference here," I said. "The reference is the Avion Electric Supply in Chicago. This letter from them says she worked there three years ago under the name of Margaret Fleer. What kind of a reference is that, sir?"

Reece's hands twitched nervously. "I know the change of names bothers you. But it's really not so involved. At the time she was working in Chicago she was married. Her married name was Fleer. When she obtained her divorce two years ago, she reverted back to her maiden name of Venus."

"Married?" I asked in a harsh voice.

"Yes, Mr. Lindsey, married. Her age on the record is twenty-one. She was married at eighteen and divorced at nineteen."

"And the Manette part?"

"I don't quite remember how she explained it. I think she said it was some sort of nickname. When girls are young

96

they seem to pick up these outlandish nicknames. You should hear some of the girls' names in this office. Sounds like an all-male chorus. Names like Billie and Jackie and Bobbie. Hers, I imagine, had the French touch—Manette. Very nice, too."

"A nickname may be nice. But not on an employment record."

"I suppose not. To tell the truth, I didn't give it a thought until now. There are so many other things I have to do."

"Didn't you ever see her social security card?"

"No. She said she lost it. But the number is down here," he said eagerly. "She remembered the number."

"This working reference is three years old, sir," I said insistently. "She must have worked since then. Did she mention Cleveland?"

"Not to me. Perhaps she was collecting alimony during that time."

"These references are too vague," I said. "A firm as large as this—"

"I'm trying to get organized," Reece said helplessly. "I can't get nearly enough skilled office helpers. I've even advertised in the Boston and Worcester papers."

"But not in the Chicago papers. It seems queer that Manette Venus would come halfway across the country to work in Danford, Massachusetts. She didn't know a soul here."

"These modern girls act so strange. I've been here several years and I don't know yet how to cope with any of them."

"Thanks, anyway, sir," I said. "Now, if you don't mind, I'd like to talk to Cole Boothbay."

"Of course. He's out in our main office behind the counter. I'll introduce you to him."

We went into the main office. There was the intermingling sound of typewriters and business machines. To the right was a large wire cage. Behind the grillwork a number of girls were busily taking packets of bills out of white canvas bags. Others were sorting coins swiftly and expertly.

"That's the payroll," Reece said. "It just came in."

"Did Manette Venus work in Payroll?" I asked.

"No. She worked in Accounts. I'd like to ask you something professional, Lindsey. How do you like our security here?"

"It looks good."

"I set it up myself," Reece said, his face beaming. "The only entrance to the building is the downstairs door. We keep it locked and guarded. We have a fire door in back of each floor. The one here leads to the fire escape. The doors are kept locked from the inside at all times. We're always careful. That's why we never had a holdup."

"Fine," I said impatiently. We were now in front of the counter. Behind it sat a good-looking man of about thirty. He had curly brown hair and a round, ruddy, apple-cheeked face. His chin was dimpled and his mouth was soft and wet. He rose up from behind a flat-topped desk and came over expectantly. Reece introduced Mr. Lindsey to Mr. Boothbay and went away. We stood there silently for a moment.

"It's about Manette Venus," I said finally.

"Which is what I thought," Boothbay said, his soft mouth spreading, grimacing. "Do you want to come inside to my desk?"

"No, I think we can talk fine out here, sir."

"Poor kid, that Manette," Boothbay said. His manner

was bland and smooth. "We really were shocked about her death. All of us here."

"Did you know her well?"

He affected a casual pose. He knew the girls in the office were watching us. He reminded me of a rooster in a barn-yard surrounded by chickens. His face was smug. He looked bored. He said, "What do you mean by 'well'?"

"She had a key to your cottage," I said evenly.

"Oh, yes. And I'm glad she wasn't murdered there. The stigma, you know—" He adjusted the thick knot of his tie. "Gad, how some girls get involved," he drawled. "But then, of all persons, you should know, shouldn't you?"

My hands itched for his neck. Instead I said very softly, "Did she ever speak of her past, sir?"

"No."

"Did you ever take her out?"

"Twice, I think. She caught my eye when she first came here. I soon found there was nothing to her. Pretty face, yes, but empty—a vacuum. Then again, I don't care to get too friendly with the office help. Leads to complications. For example, I invited the office help to my camp. Gave them a break. They lead such drab, dull lives, you know. They didn't appreciate it. It was a waste of time."

"Manette was there those times?"

"Yes. Though she'd rather we'd been there alone. She had a crush on me, I suppose. Always phoning me at my flat."

I wanted to punch his conceited nose. I took a deep breath and said, "Did she have any girl friends in the office? For example, somebody she could borrow a car from?"

"No, she had no girl friends here. One Saturday morning

she borrowed *my* car. I have a gray convertible. She said she wanted to use it for a few hours. I let her. I've always been a soft touch."

"Did she ever mention a Helen Toledo?"

His fingers drummed on the counter. "No."

"You've been here over a year, Mr. Boothbay?"

"Fourteen months."

"You're a native of Danford?"

"No, I'm from New York."

"You're an accountant?"

"I work as an accounting assistant. I have a B. A. in economics. Our Mr. Reece hasn't. What do you think of the old poop?"

"I don't know," I said.

"Who do you think really runs this office? I do. We'd be better off if the charitable Mr. Staley paid the old poop his salary and told him to stay home. All old Fulton does is clutter up a perfectly good office."

"That's Mr. Staley's business," I said. "Where do you live now, Mr. Boothbay?"

"In Danford. At 176 Crescent Avenue. It's an old converted town house. My flat is on the third floor. It's one of those ancient places with a fireplace in every room. There's not much better in a crummy mill town like Danford."

"Thanks," I said. "That's all, sir." It wasn't really what I wanted to say to him. But the Commissioner was always strict about courtesy.

I came outside and climbed into the cruiser. I picked up the handphone and signaled Troop E that I was back on the air. I started the motor. I was thinking of Manette Venus and of all the lies she had told me in so short a time.

I drove through the gate, waving to the guard. Just outside I almost collided with a black sedan coming in. The sedan's horn tooted twice. I stopped. I saw Ed Newpole step out. He came over to my window.

"You working out here, Ralph?"

"In a way," I said. "This is one of my patrols."

He cocked his head sideways like a bird. "Inside the mill?"

"All right," I said. "So I was in there asking questions."

"About what, Ralph?"

I told him. When I was finished there was a hurt look on his face. He said, "We do those things systematically, Ralph. If I'd have wanted you to ask questions in there, I'd have told you."

"I'm sorry," I said. "I guess I'm a little overanxious."

"I know. And maybe it's my fault for not explaining it to you. From now on we'd better work together. I'm staying at the Hotel Danford Terrace. You'll check in and take a room there. You'll move out of the barracks now. I've already spoken to Captain Walsh."

I nodded my head. "There's something else, Lieutenant. How *is* she?"

"You mean Ellen?"

"Yes."

"Well, I saw her in court." He scratched the end of his nose lugubriously. "It happened. They arraigned her for murder and remanded her to the county jail without bail. You had to expect it, Ralph."

"I've got to see her, Lieutenant."

"Not yet, Ralph," he said. "Let it rest awhile."

"She doesn't want to see me?"

"Her pride's been hurt. You walked out on her and took

up with Manette. And her folks—well—they kind of blame you for everything that's happened."

"They should," I said bitterly. "I blame myself, too."

"I'm not so sure where the blame lies. And I'm not too satisfied with the evidence, either." He smiled cheerily. "We'll dig into it, you and I and Chet Granger. Maybe we'll find something."

"When do I start?"

"You're real anxious, ain't you?"

"Yes, sir. More than anxious."

"All right, you can start with Helen Toledo. I think she knows more than she's been telling."

CHAPTER 10 _____

IN Danford, three blocks over from Main, there was a honky-tonk section. Here the varicolored neon signs were lighted in broad daylight. In the middle of the block there was a row of cheap cafés and beer parlors. I parked the black cruiser assigned to me, and went in under the red neon sign that said *Starlight Café*.

The place was in semidarkness and almost empty. A ceiling fan turned slowly. There was a smell of stale beer and stale cigar smoke and frying onions. A fat, dirty-aproned bartender leaned on a dark, ancient bar, talking to a man in dungarees. The man put down a foam-circled beer glass and wiped his mouth with the back of his hand.

Sitting in a corner booth was a buxom girl with flaming, artifically colored red hair. She was wearing a blue waitress uniform. She was leaning forward over the table while a grimy, unshaven man whispered in her ear. Suddenly she threw her head back and laughed raucously.

I came up to the edge of the bar and the bartender moved over to meet me. I said, "I'm looking for Helen Toledo."

The bartender moved his head slightly. "There in the booth."

"I'd like someplace where I can talk to her alone." I took out my badge and showed it. The bartender stared down at it, then his eyes came up unhappily.

"Anything wrong, Trooper?"

"No, sir. I just want to talk to Helen Toledo."

The bartender wiped damp hands on his apron. "Sure. There's an office out back. You go in there. I'll send Helen in. I ain't going to insult you by offering you whisky. But if you want a nice cold bottle of ale on the house—"

"Just Helen," I said shortly.

I sat behind a dirty, littered table that served as a desk. I moved a spindle stacked with bills and waited. A shadow moved along the wall and Helen Toledo came in.

"Hi," she said. "You're a cop, huh?"

"Ralph Lindsey," I said. "State Police."

"Ah," she said. She surveyed me. She sat down. Her mascara was heavy and her eyelids blued, and she was over thirty years old. She had voluptuous hips and she moved them from side to side as she adjusted her position in the chair. She tugged at her girdle. "Honestly," she said confidentially, "I must be getting fat. I was built when meat was cheap and I got to watch my weight all the time."

"You look fine," I said.

"Thanks, kid. You got a cigarette on you?"

I took out my pack and handed it over. She picked out

one, wet it with the tip of her tongue and put it in her mouth. I leaned over and lit it for her.

"It's a chance to grab a smoke," she said, taking the cigarette from her mouth and exhaling. "It don't look good for me to be smoking out there," she added virtuously. She ran her tongue over the bright carmine of her lips. "So you're Ralph Lindsey, huh? You was in the papers this morning."

"I know."

"Manette used to mention you."

"What did she say?"

"Nothing much—except that she fell for you like a ton of bricks. You fishing for something about her?"

"Yes," I said. "We want to know where she came from. Her family, her past. Miss Toledo, did she ever talk to you about those things?"

"She never told me nothing."

"You met her here at the café, Miss Toledo. How?"

She took a deep drag on the cigarette and blew the smoke out. "Manette comes in here alone one night. About a month ago. I serve her an orange blossom. Then she gives me a song-and-dance about being alone in the big city. Me and my big heart, I feel sorry for the kid. So I meet her outside after work and we go to an eating place. Then another time she phoned me and we went to a picture show. A couple of times I went to the house where she lived and we had a hen party. Then last week she meets you. It beats me how quick she changed. Brother, from then on she wants to talk about you all the time. I see she don't need me any more, so I keep away. That's all. Last night a cop comes to see me and says Manette was knocked off by some dame. Hey, was I surprised! I hadn't seen Manette for two-three days."

"She didn't phone you or anything?"

"No. She always was a moody kid."

"Maybe she had a reason," I said. "Maybe she was in some kind of trouble."

Helen Toledo was pensive for a moment, the blue tobacco smoke curling up from her nostrils. "Sure, something was eating her the whole time I knew her. But don't ask me what, because Manette didn't talk about nothing but you and the weather."

"Not even Cole Boothbay?"

"Who's he?"

"Nobody special," I said. "What's your home address, Miss Toledo?"

"It ain't the YWCA."

I grinned. "I didn't think so."

"I live at the Regal," she said defensively. "It's cheap but it's clean."

"All right," I said. "Thanks, Miss Toledo."

"The name's Helen. Don't be so damn formal."

I grinned again. "Okay, Helen."

She smiled back. "You going to be around town for a while?"

"I'll be in and out."

"Where you staying?"

"I'm at the Hotel Danford Terrace."

"It's the best dump in this dumpy town. I might look you up sometime, Ralph. If you don't mind going out with an older girl."

"I don't mind."

106

"If you've got nothing to do some night, I know a few places we can go and get some laughs."

"Sure," I said. "Thanks."

She laughed. "See? I make my own dates. I don't horse around. If I like a guy I tell him right out. And I like you, kid. I liked you the minute you walked in." She stood up and tugged at her girdle again. "I'd better get back outside before Gus blows a gasket. Gus is the bartender. He's boss of this broken-down joint."

I was in my room at the Hotel Danford Terrace. It was after supper and outside it had grown completely dark. There was a knock at my door and I went over and opened it. Ed Newpole came in. He was carrying a zippered leather portfolio. He took off his hat and sank down in the lounge chair. His face was pinched with fatigue.

"You doing your report?" he asked.

"Yes," I said. "But I'm afraid it was a waste of time." Then I told him about Helen Toledo.

"Nothing's wasted," he said. He unlaced his shoes, took them off and wiggled his stocking feet.

"Manette was a sweet, refined kid," I said. "I just can't picture her with Helen Toledo. It doesn't make sense."

Newpole grunted. His eyes spotted my pipe and tobacco pouch on the desk. "You smoke a pipe?" he asked.

"Whenever I have a little time. I brought it from home this trip."

He took out a pipe with a discolored meerschaum bowl. "What kind of tobacco do you use?"

"A rough cut." I tossed him the pouch. He opened it, sniffed, and tamped tobacco into the bowl of his pipe. He lit it and puffed. "Good," he said. "Sweet as a nut. Sweet

107

like Manette Venus. There's a sweet, refined kid from Chicago. She was married at eighteen, divorced at nineteen. Suddenly she shows up in Danford for no reason at all. Why an old mill town like Danford?"

"I don't know, Lieutenant."

"This sweet, refined girl goes to one of the toughest bars in town and makes friends with a chippy named Helen Toledo. Later this sweet, refined girl goes to another bar and picks up a state cop in civilian clothes. She asks him too many questions. The bartender says the girl had never been in there before."

"All right, so she went in there deliberately to pick me up. I've been thinking that, too."

"Good. You're learning." Newpole stretched his legs. "After the girl gets to know you, suddenly she wants to pull up stakes and leave town. She's scared of something, and maybe she's buying herself a little protection in you. The sweet, refined girl carries a gun. She says your life is in danger, too, but she don't say why. She thinks a man is watching her from a parked car on Glen Road and she almost throws a fit. Finally, she says she's going to come clean with you. But before she has the chance she's killed. And that, my boy, is only the beginning."

He unzipped his leather case and brought out a blue perforated teletype message. "Here's a TT from the Chicago police. The girl's got still another name. Her maiden name was Margaret Venable, not Venus."

"Go on," I said, my voice clogging in my throat. "I don't know what to believe now."

"I have more," Newpole said. "The girl was married at eighteen to a man named Andrew Fleer. Fleer was twenty-five. A year after they were married, Fleer was convicted of attempted blackmail and got from one to three. Manette, or Margaret, was indicted on the same charge. But she skipped her bail. She went to Juarez, Mexico, and got a quickie divorce from Fleer. Then they lost her trail. The Chicago cops still have a flyer out on her."

"It doesn't add up," I said tonelessly. "If you had known her—"

"This is a positive identification, Ralph. There's no mistake. Fleer served his year, did his parole stretch and disappeared from Illinois."

"You said attempted blackmail. What was it?"

"One of the oldest touches in the world. The badger game. The girl meets an older, married man and invites him to her room. Just when they get comfortable, her husband comes busting in. The older man don't want any scandal, naturally. So he pays off." Newpole scratched his toes. "But this time the Fleers had an old duffer who didn't scare. He promised to pay off the next day. When Manette and Fleer went to the meeting place, cops were staked out there. They grabbed the Fleers."

"Did they have a previous record?"

"Not the girl. Andrew Fleer was a smalltime grifter. He'd been in a few shenanigans, but managed to stay out of jail. I said they were from Chicago. But they weren't, not originally. They came from the cornbelt. Some small college town in Iowa called Ames. Fleer was a student there, studying under the G. I. bill. Manette was living with an old aunt. The aunt died. Manette—we should call her Margaret—married Fleer and left town. She had no kin. That's her life, kid. It's not sweet and refined, is it?"

"No," I said. I took my pipe from the desk and began to

fill it with uncertain fingers. There was a rap on the door. Newpole slipped into his shoes, got up and opened it. Lieutenant Chet Granger came into the room.

He smiled diffidently. "Everybody gets in early except me." He sat down and crossed his long legs.

"Well?" Newpole asked him. "How are you coming along with the Reeces?"

Granger put a stick of gum in his mouth. "This Fulton Reece might not have any money, but he's old family and still belongs to the best clubs. There's one called the Danford Pioneers and they have a dinner once a month. The Reeces were there last night and they've got top witnesses to prove it."

"So?" Newpole said, puffing on his pipe.

"So I went down to Danford Police Headquarters to see if they had a record on Reece. Not that I expected to find anything. He came from a prominent family and nobody in Danford would put him on record anyway." His jaw moved over his gum for a moment. "I didn't find anything, so I started to ask around. You know, shooting the breeze with some of the old-time cops. They buttoned up on me. But I did find something. There was an old-timer who did a little talking. Leo Nason. You know him?"

Newpole shook his head.

"An old harness cop," Granger said. "Now he's like a custodian. Nason told me he made a pinch about 1902. He was only a rookie cop then in a big helmet and a frock coat."

"Cripes, what a memory," Newpole said.

"This the old-timer remembered. He put the pinch on Fulton Reece. Reece was ten, twelve years old then. Reece had killed a horse."

110

"A horse?" Newpole asked.

"Not really a horse. A Shetland pony. This Reece was living in a big house in town then. Next door was another big house and a girl lived there about Reece's age. The girl owned a pony and a cart, and Fulton was jealous. And little girls being little girls, she gave Fulton a bad time over it. So one night Reece sneaked over there with a big butcher knife and slit the girl's pony from ear to ear."

Newpole said, "And he was only ten or twelve years old then?"

"Sure. The girl called the cops and Leo Nason came. He, being a rookie, brought them down to the station, instead of sending the station to them. The whole thing was hushed up quick. The Reece family paid for the pony."

"Well," Newpole said, putting his pipe down, "the guy's a character, all right."

"Here's more," Granger said. "This afternoon I hung around the gate at Staley Woolen. When Reece came out at five I tailed him. He drove out to a plush roadhouse on the pike called *Conti's*. There, in a corner of the foyer, he meets a platinum blond chick. She don't look more than sixteen. He stays with her a few minutes. Doesn't even buy a cup of coffee. He leaves her and goes out. I followed him home." His teeth masticated the gum. "I don't know what to make of it, Ed. There's something wrong with the picture. If Reece was a sharp dresser with a waxed mustache and a leer, I could see it. But a sloppy old man like him doesn't go together with a platinum blonde."

Newpole was lacing his shoes with a thoughtful expression on his face. He stood up.

"We'll work tonight," he said.

111

I started to put my report away. Newpole said, "Not you, Ralph. Just Chet and I. We're breaking you in easy at first. You rest up and get some sleep. Check with me the first thing in the morning."

CHAPTER 11 _____

I went to Ed Newpole's room early the next morning. There were heavy wrinkles in his face and his eyes were red-rimmed and droopy. He was in his undershirt and trousers. Chet Granger came out of the bathroom. His hair was wet and combed. His face was freshly shaven and there were flecks of talcum powder near his ears.

"We got in only a couple of hours ago," Newpole said to me. He took out a fresh shirt from a bureau drawer and tore off the blue paper band. He pointed to a large Manila envelope on the chair. There were globs of red sealing wax on it. "There's the evidence on the Venus case. Chet is bringing it into Boston. Meanwhile, we've got a job for you."

He motioned to me to sit down. He said, "We were at the Regal Hotel last night. Helen Toledo has a regular visitor there. A man named Al Yekiti. Ever hear of him?"

I shook my head.

"This Yekiti is a torpedo with a record as long as your arm. Mostly armed robbery, assaults, stick-ups."

Granger went over to the bureau and picked up his tie. "We sent Al away a couple of times."

Newpole said, "The man is bad. I mean, nasty bad. In a holdup he'll take the victim's money, then beat him up, break his teeth, even if there's no resistance. The man is vicious. No conscience, nothing. Just senseless meanness. He serves his time and comes out again. One thing about him. When he comes out of the pen, he doesn't wait long before he pulls another job. We'd like to find out what it is before it happens. Maybe we can save some poor shop-keeper from being killed."

"If you picked him up and questioned him—" I said.

Granger knotted his tie. "Hell, Yekiti wouldn't tell you what color shoes he's wearing."

Newpole buttoned his shirt and stuffed it into his trousers. "So now we may have a tie-in between Helen Toledo, Al Yekiti and Manette Venus. We know the Venus girl has worked the badger game." He cocked his head at me. "Did you ever think Manette was ready to make a proposition to you?"

"You mean a criminal proposition?"

"Yes."

"I've thought of it," I said.

"Seems like a perfect setup to me," Newpole said. "I imagine she could show the hip to one of these old farmers and get him out to some tourist cabin. Then, just at the right time, a uniformed state trooper walks in on them. That would scare any man to death. He'd pay any amount of money."

114

He turned and looked at me. I was staring morosely at the rug.

"Disillusioned, huh?" he said. "Sure, she looked like a sweet, innocent kid. But I'll show you pictures of the nicest looking criminals you ever saw. Anyway, we've checked on Helen Toledo. She ain't as bad as Manette Venus. Her record shows disorderly conduct, drunk and disorderly, nothing much."

"What do you want me to do?"

"I want you to tail Yekiti," Newpole said. "I'll give you his address and his car registration number. Watch what he does, where he goes. If you see him carrying anything suspicious, anything that looks like a weapon, shake him down. Otherwise leave him alone. He's big and he's mean. If you have to go up against him, watch yourself."

"Yes, sir," I said.

"I'm going to try to be near," Newpole said. "But I've got some other things to do. If you get jammed up, protect yourself in the clinches. Yekiti doesn't use any rules."

The morning sun was warm and a vagrant breeze stirred the papers in the gutter. In front of the seedy, ramshackle boardinghouse there was a black, late-model sedan. One window had a cracked glass held together by adhesive tape. The upholstery was soiled and grease-stained. I stood in an alley between two stores watching the house and the car. I had been there two hours and my legs kept getting numb. Each time I would shift them, stamping my feet, sending the nerves tingling again. The sun climbed and I could feel the heat of its rays on the back of my neck. A fat woman went by wheeling a baby carriage, her body soft and shapeless, her stockings wrinkled.

I waited. A delivery truck went by, milk cases rattling, leaving a trail of melting ice water. A Danford police car came slowly by, the two patrolmen lolling in the front seat, coats unbuttoned, faces listless in the Indian summer heat. A young matron walked by the alley, her heels clicking on the pavement, her arms full of bundles, her hips wigwagging under the weight. Then the front door of the rooming house opened.

I stood there rigid and motionless as Al Yekiti shuffled down the stairs. He wore a blue windbreaker and no hat. He was a huge, hulking man, with a hairy unclean skin. He had long apelike arms, the fingers extending like bananas on a stalk. He stood on the curb, a cigarette dangling from his mouth. He looked up and down the street. I squeezed back further into the shadows.

Yekiti got into his car and started off. I sprinted for the black cruiser. I slid in, gunned the motor and turned out after him.

Yekiti drove uptown, through the traffic of Main Street and three blocks over. He parked the car in front of the Starlight Café. I drove by swiftly, turned the corner and stepped out. Yekiti was gone. I walked down the block and crossed the street. There was a small luncheonette with fly-specked window and fly-specked signs. I went inside, sat down at the counter near the window and ordered coffee.

I could see the entrance of the Starlight Café and only cool darkness beyond. But the sun was hitting the corner of the Starlight's plate glass window, sending its rays into the corner booth. I saw Yekiti move in there and sit down. Two other men got into the booth. They were young, with hard, vicious faces and long, unkempt hair. Helen Toledo moved into view. She was carrying three drinks on a brown plastic tray. She bent over Yekiti and patted his head. I could see Yekiti laugh. He nudged one of the men, then put his arm around Helen. She swung around, put the drinks down, then disappeared from view.

My coffee came and I put sugar in, stirring it, tasting it. The coffee was muddy, stale and bitter, and the cup had a grimy rim. I put it down on the counter. I looked across the street. Yekiti was hunched over the booth, whispering, poking out a large finger at the men for emphasis. He grabbed his liquor glass and gulped his drink. I toyed with my coffee. The counterman was eyeing me curiously. I stood up, threw a dime down, and sauntered out. Next door there was a second-hand clothing store. I peered in the window, using its reflection as a mirror.

Al Yekiti came out of the Starlight Café. In his hand I saw a brown paper package. It was cylindrical, about fifteen inches long and four inches in diameter.

Yekiti went for his car. I moved fast. I cut across the street behind him, turned the corner and got into the cruiser. I turned it around, caught up with Yekiti two blocks away and fell in behind.

Yekiti drove back to his rooming house. He parked his car at the curb, took his package and went inside. I pulled up behind him, left the cruiser and ran up to the door. I opened it. There was a dark, musty hallway.

I could hear Yekiti's heavy tread on the stairs above me. I went up on my toes, swiftly. I caught him at the door of his room.

He turned fast. His big awkward appearance had been deceiving. He was lithe and quick. But before he had swung halfway around, I was on him. I grabbed him by the back of his collar and yanked the windbreaker down hard. It threw him off balance. He dropped the package.

"What the hell is this?" he grunted. He lurched into me, hitting me hard with his shoulder.

"State Police," I said. I grabbed his arm.

"You crazy nut," he rumbled. "Who you think you're kidding?" He swung his other arm in the narrow quarters. His fist came up with swift force, sideswiping my mouth, glancing off. I bore in again, twisting one arm up behind his back, pinning the other with my body. A strong smell of liquor mingled with his rank body odor. Yekiti swore under his breath, trying to free his arms.

I heard the downstairs' front door open and a figure came up the stairs toward us. I let go of Yekiti and moved away, backtracking. I reached for my hip holster and brought out the gun.

Yekiti, moving for me, stopped and looked at the gun. He brought his hands up slowly.

"Ralph," the figure on the stairs called. I recognized the voice of Lieutenant Ed Newpole.

"I'm here," I said. "I've got Yekiti."

He came bounding up the stairs. Yekiti dropped his hands. "Hell," he said disgustedly. "It's Newpole, the state cop."

Newpole pushed him against the wall and patted his clothes. He ran quick, expert hands down the legs. He pushed Yekiti away. "All right, Al," he said. "Can we go inside?"

"Sure," Yekiti said. "I got nothing to hide."

He unlocked his door. I put my gun away and picked up the package.

It was a small, dirty room. There were empty beer cans

on the floor and soiled clothing strewn about. I gave the
package to Newpole. He hefted it. Then he tore the wrap-
ping off.

It was a large salami. Yekiti sat down and began to laugh.
He rocked back and forth in the chair, slapping his hands
on his knees, bull-like roars coming out of him.

I looked stupidly at Newpole. Newpole's lean face was
impassive. I could feel cold perspiration on my body. Newpole sniffed. The windows were closed and the place had a
fetid odor.

Yekiti stopped laughing. He wiped his eyes with the back
of his hand. "You really got some slap-happy cops," he said
to Newpole. "How long's this kid been around? Or does he
think I'll shoot somebody with a salami?"

Newpole said nothing. He went by Yekiti and looked
into the single closet. He went to the bureau and opened
the drawers. He rummaged through. He closed the drawers.
He went to the bed, pulled the sheets and mattress back
and looked at the dusty springs. He felt the pillow and the
mattress ticking. He stood back and surveyed the room.

"You find it?" Yekiti asked.

Newpole shook his head sadly. "What do you think I was
looking for, Al?"

"A gun," Yekiti said. "The hell with you, Lieutenant. I
ain't got a gun."

"Now that's no way to talk, Al," Newpole said softly.
"You're losing your manners."

"The hell with you," Yekiti chanted. "The hell with you,
the hell with you."

Newpole smiled at him. Yekiti lumbered to his feet and
stared at him, fixedly, like a bull in a pasture.

"What are you doing in Danford?" Newpole asked him.

"I'm only gonna answer questions I'm supposed to. I know my rights, Newpole."

"What are you doing in Danford?" Newpole asked again. "Or do I get down to your level and stop acting like a gentleman?"

"I live here now," Newpole said.

"Where do you work?"

"I'm a part-time loader in a warehouse."

"What warehouse, Al?"

"Reach Forwarding Company."

"Where were you Thursday night, Al?"

Yekiti's brows came down in thought. "Thursday night I was at the Starlight. All night. You can ask Gus, the bartender."

"And I can ask Helen Toledo, too. What are you doing with her?"

"The hell with you. That's my business."

"What's the score on Manette Venus?"

"Who dat?"

"Don't waste your wisecracks on me, Al," Newpole said. "Manette Venus, alias Margaret Venable, alias Margaret Fleer."

"A long one, huh?" Yekiti said. "Who dat?"

Newpole turned to me. "Where was he today?"

"At the Starlight Café," I said. "He was in a booth with two men."

Newpole scratched his nose. "Who were your two friends, Al?"

"Dick Calvaris and Bill Horace. A couple of old pals."

"Nice boys, both of them. What were you doing? Getting up a game of checkers?"

"Nothing. I run into them. We had a few drinks to-gether."

"What's the new scheme, Al?"

"Who dat?"

"The plan. The job you're going to pull."

"You bother me, Lieutenant."

"Hurry up and get it over with, Al. Because this time when we grab you you'll probably go up for good."

Yekiti spat on the floor and rubbed the spittle with his shoe. "You got to catch 'em first, Lieutenant."

"You're easy to catch, Al. Catching you is as easy as waking up in the morning."

Yekiti sneered, scratched his black mop of hair, then looked down at his black-rimmed fingernails. "Keep talking. I got nothing else to do but listen to you."

"We're through for now," Newpole said. "But we'll see you, Al."

"The hell with you," Yekiti said.

We went out of there. We came outside and stood there in the bright sun. Newpole scuffed his shoe against the pavement.

"It's not good," he said in a flat, weary voice. "We had to go and tip our hand. He's going to be more careful now."

"It's my fault," I said disconsolately, rubbing my bruised mouth. "I got all excited when I saw the package. I thought it was a sawed-off shotgun."

"I can't blame you. I might have done the same thing myself." He grinned suddenly. "Who'd have thought he was carrying a salami, anyway?"

"I get too anxious," I said. "I keep thinking of Ellen. The D. A. is going to do everything to convict her."

"Which is his job. Don't forget, you're on the same side of the fence he is."

"I'm going to forget it one of these days."

"I don't think so. I had a little talk with Fred Walsh about you. He thinks some day you'll be doing the right things."

"Not Walsh," I said. "Walsh has no use for me. He tolerates me because of my old man."

"No, he says you've got the instinct for police work. He told me about something when you were with the troop only a month. Something about a gas station burglary on the turnpike. Told me to ask you about it some day. What was it, Ralph?"

"It wasn't much," I said. "The station was having some trouble with breaking and entering. It was small stuff. Almost every night somebody would break in and take a few tires. The old chief in the town staked himself out in the gas station a couple of nights. Nothing happened. So he stopped. They broke in again and took some more tires. So the chief called Troop E for help. Captain Walsh sent me out.

"If you stopped and thought about it you had to know it was local boys. Because the thieves knew every move the chief made. So I drove into the little town and cruised around. On one side street I spotted a boy about fourteen years old. The boy saw the state cruiser and started to run. I jumped out and grabbed him. I said, 'All right, where did you hide those tires?' And the boy said, 'They're in my cellar.' And that's where they were."

"You never saw the kid before in your life?" Newpole asked.

"No. But when he started to run—"

Newpole chuckled. "I get a kick out of it. You muckled onto that kid and asked him the right question. That's what I call instinct. Not many have it."

"It was more luck than anything," I said. "I'm surprised Captain Walsh still remembers it."

"He remembers everything, that guy. He's got a mind like a filing cabinet." Newpole looked at his watch. "I had a reason for looking for you. I asked Cole Boothbay to come to the barracks for an interview. And I want you there to check on what he told you before. We'd better get going."

CHAPTER 12 _____

COLE BOOTHBAY was wearing a well-tailored gray tweed suit. He sat in a chair in Captain Walsh's office and crossed his legs comfortably. His liquid brown eyes had a bantering look in them. Captain Walsh hitched up his chair and looked stoically at my swollen lip. Ed Newpole took out his pipe and filled it slowly. He lit it and puffed. He said, "Purely routine, Mr. Boothbay. A few things we want to clear up."

"Anything, Lieutenant," Boothbay said.

Newpole said, "You told Patrolman Lindsey you lived in New York. Where in New York, Mr. Boothbay?"

"But I never told Lindsey I lived in New York," Boothbay said blandly. "I lived in Hoboken."

"How many years?"

"Off and on, all my life, Lieutenant."

"But you worked in New York."

"Yes. The Signet Crest Company. Five years."

"Doing what?"

"Accounting."

"What kind of company is it?"

"Import-export, Lieutenant."

"They still in business?"

"Yes, I think so. In a small way."

"Why did you leave them, Mr. Boothbay?"

"It was a small company. In all modesty, I was a bit too good for them, and they couldn't afford to pay me what I was worth. They were handling war surplus stuff, and materials were getting less and less. Then I saw an ad from Staley Woolen. They needed accounting assistants. So I came here and got a job."

"Were you ever in Chicago?" Newpole asked.

"No, Lieutenant."

"Let's talk about Manette Venus," Newpole said. "Did she ever come to your apartment on Crescent Avenue?"

Boothbay smiled. "She was there. Once."

"There were others who came there?"

"A few others," Boothbay said, a slight smirk on his face.

"Girls from your office?"

"Yes." Boothbay looked up, his eyes amused. "You won't want their names, will you? It isn't cricket."

"We're interested only in Manette Venus," Newpole said coldly. "How many times did she go with you to the cottage on Deer Pond? And I mean just the two of you."

"A few times."

"When did the affair stop?"

"When she met Patrolman Lindsey. I broke it off then."

"*You* broke it off? Why?"

"After all, we *were* having a clandestine affair, Manette and I. Frankly, I always considered discretion the better part of valor. I couldn't see myself tangling with a big husky trooper."

"Did she try to get you to change your mind?"

"Yes. She said she needed him for something temporarily. After that we could resume where we left off. But I was through with her."

"Did she tell you why she needed him?"

"No. And I never ask a lady personal questions."

"Didn't you feel any attachment to Miss Venus?"

"No, she interested me no longer. I was beginning to get bored. It was an interlude for me, that's all. I'm very philosophical about girls."

"If you were so intimate with her," Newpole said, "you must have known about her background."

"Not a thing. I wasn't interested. I knew she came from out west, nothing more."

"Where were you the night she died?"

"At the movies."

"Alone?"

Boothbay raised his eyebrows slightly. "Yes. Why?"

"Nothing," Newpole said, a muscle twitching in his jaw. "It's just that you're such a big man with the women, I didn't think they'd let you spend even one night alone."

Boothbay laughed. "Ah, touché, Lieutenant. Touché. Very good, I must say."

Newpole's nostrils dilated. "So you went to a movie that night. Can you prove it?"

"I have a ticket stub."

"Do you always save your ticket stub?"

"Always. I'm a fanatical ticket-stub collector."

"What time did the movie start, Mr. Boothbay?"

"Eight o'clock."

"Manette Venus was killed about seven-thirty. You'd have time to get to Glen Road before the show started."

"To give Miss Levesque moral aid and suasion? Ah, but I had no reason to assist Miss Levesque. Certainly less reason than your own Patrolman Lindsey. And what's more, I didn't leave the house until seven forty-five. It was a neighborhood theater. The Oriental."

"Did anybody see you leave the house, Mr. Boothbay?"

"I don't remember offhand."

Newpole puffed on his pipe. He picked up some papers from the desk and shuffled through them. Then he said, "Okay, Mr. Boothbay. I think that's all for now." He turned to Captain Walsh. "Unless you have some questions, Captain."

"A few," Walsh said in a flat even voice. "Mr. Boothbay, did you ever see Ralph Lindsey before?"

"Yesterday, Captain. He came to the factory and asked questions."

"You never met him before then?"

"No, sir, I did not."

"Did you ever see Manette Venus with him?"

"No, Captain. I never bumped into them together. Until yesterday I had no idea what he looked like."

"That's all," Captain Walsh said tersely. "Thank you."

Boothbay stood up. He picked up his topcoat that was draped over the chair. He flipped his hand airily at us and went out.

Captain Walsh watched him go. He got up and pushed his chair back. He looked at me. "Your shoes need a shine," he said. "The minute a man gets away from the troop for a

127

day, he gets careless. Shine 'em up, Lindsey." Then he turned to Newpole. "What do you think of Cole Boothbay, Ed?"

"Boothbay?" Newpole said. "I think he's a damn liar."

CHAPTER 13 _____

I was sitting in my hotel room in my shirt sleeves, nibbling at my pencil, bent forward, working on my report. It was eight o'clock at night and I was alone. Lieutenant Chet Granger was in Boston, and Ed Newpole was out working somewhere. I was finishing the report and listening to a girl vocalist on the radio at the same time.

There was a light tap on my door. I wasn't sure what it was at first. Then the tap came again. I laid the pencil down and put the report in the desk drawer. The knock came again, a bit sharper. I went over and opened up.

Helen Toledo stood in the hallway swinging the straps of her handbag. She was wearing a wide-brimmed blue hat, a blue polka dot dress and a pink wool shortcoat. Her shoes were blue sandals with very high cork soles and heels.

"Hi." She smiled, opening her brightly painted mouth, but the smile was forced and mechanical. She said nervously, "Can I come in?"

I stood aside. She came in and closed the door. She tried to smile again, this time provocatively. Again she failed. There was a grotesqueness about her. She was a parody in cheap finery.

She sat down in the lounge chair. She said, "I was passing by. I thought maybe you could stand some company."

"Sure," I said. "I like company."

"You got anything to drink, kid?"

"No. But I'll send down for something. What would you like?"

She smiled archly. "Usually I have myself a couple of gin drinks. But when I'm with a gentleman my tastes run to Scotch."

I smiled back at her. We were like two animals stalking each other. I picked up the telephone and called room service.

Helen Toledo sank back in her chair. "Nice music," she commented. She smoked a king-size cigarette, taken from a garish, enameled cigarette case. She crossed her legs with deliberate carelessness. "It's been a warm day," she said.

"Yes," I said. "How's your friend, Al Yekiti?"

"How did you know Al's a friend of mine?"

"Simple. We asked Al. He told us."

"Ah," she said, staring at me, her face perplexed. She blew smoke from her mouth. "Al's all right. He's a big ox and he ain't too smart, but—" She stopped suddenly and looked over at the desk, seeing the pencil and a sheet of hotel stationery. "You writing letters?" she asked coyly.

"I'm finished," I said. "What were you saying about Al?"

"Nothing. Who wants to talk about Al? You look more of a sport to me. You come to town much?"

"Often enough."

130

"They put you with the detectives, huh? You must be working on something big and special."

"Everything is special, Helen," I said.

There was a knock at the door and I went over and opened it. The bellman brought in a tray of drinks. I tipped him, paid the check and sent him away.

She snuffed out her cigarette in the ash tray. She picked up her glass and said, "Here's luck."

She drank. She put her glass down on the table beside her. "You didn't touch yours," she said.

"Go ahead," I said. "I enjoy watching somebody else."

"You haven't been a cop long, have you?"

"Not long."

"You look like a sharp kid," she said. "Too sharp to be a cop." She sipped on her drink. I waited for her to go on.

She said, "A real sharp kid can make a buck in this town."

"Yes," I said. "How sharp does he have to be?"

"He's got to know his way around." Her eyelids came down slowly and up again. "A trooper's pay don't go far these days. A guy's got to be interested enough to make a dollar on the outside. He wouldn't be hurting nobody, either. But, as I say, a guy's really got to be interested."

I picked up my glass and put it down again without drinking.

"I'm just making conversation, get me?" she said. "But if I find me the right guy, we could make some money together. It would be a safe, sure operation, fast and foolproof. In and out. One job and break clean."

"You're asking if I'm interested, Helen?"

"I ain't asking anybody, kid. Like I said, I'm just making small talk."

"Who else is in on it?"

131

"You interested or curious?"

"I might be interested. Who else is in on it?"

"I got friends."

"Al Yekiti? Calvaris and Horace?"

"I said I got friends. I didn't say who."

"I'm still listening," I said. "I haven't walked away."

She smiled. Her eyes became half-lidded. "Don't be foolish, kid. Nobody shows their cards until the pot is called. What kind of poker player are you, anyway?"

"I might want to buy a few chips. I might want to get into the game."

"You'd have to show me, kid."

"How?"

"We got ways. They might want to test you first, get your feet wet. But once you're in, you're in. You can't turn around and walk away. Somebody else tried it." She drew her hand across her throat in a quick gesture. "That person ain't around any more."

"Manette Venus," I said slowly.

"Maybe," she said. "I warned her. I told her what was going to happen to her."

"You knew Manette Venus was going to be killed," I said softly.

"I didn't mention Manette Venus," she said smugly. "You did." Then she caught the expression on my face. "Say, what's the matter with you?"

"Manette Venus," I said. "The house on Glen Road. Ellen Levesque walked into something there. Manette Venus was already tagged."

She jumped up, overturning her glass. The liquor splashed onto the table and the glass rolled to the rug.

132

"Hey, look," she said, alarmed. "I was just kidding. A joke—"

"No," I said. "You were in on Manette's murder."

"Are you crazy?" she shouted. "Who gave you such a nutty idea? I'm getting out of this booby hatch."

"Where are you going, Helen?"

"Away from you, Trooper. You got some buttons missing. I was having a little fun with you. But you've got a crazy imagination."

"We'll go together," I said, tightening my tie knot and slipping into my jacket. "You and I. I want you to see what a State Police barracks looks like."

"You're kidding," she said faintly, dry-mouthed. "Why, the whole thing was a big gag. Can't you take a joke, kid?"

"I like jokes," I said. "I can't stop from laughing over this one. Maybe you can make the captain laugh, too."

"Look, you're not a bad guy," she said earnestly. "From the beginning I had you pegged for a sport. I've been level with you."

"No," I said. "You've lied about Manette Venus. The way you met her, everything. But tonight I was getting some of the truth. Come on, we're wasting time."

"I'm not going with you to no barracks," she said, heading for the door.

I moved ahead of her and blocked it. "Then I'll have to make you go, Helen. I'm arresting you on suspicion of murder."

"But you don't understand," she said brokenly. "They see me come out with you and they'll kill me."

"There's somebody waiting outside?"

"No, no. I'm alone. Look, let me go. Give me a break."

"The same break you gave Manette Venus," I said. I motioned her to the door.

Her face was pasty and she seemed physically ill now. She went unsteadily to the door, wobbling on her platform sandals. "I'm as good as dead," she said dully. "Just as good as dead."

I opened the door and looked out into the hallway. It was empty. I held the door for her. She came out and we went to the elevators. The elevator came up and the door opened. Helen Toledo was crying softly, the mascara ooz-ing down her cheeks in black wavy lines. The elevator operator tried not to look at her.

We came down to the lobby. We went through. I walked slightly behind her. Outside, on the sidewalk, I said, "The cruiser is at the corner."

She made a quick half-step as though to run. I grabbed her wrist. "It's foolish," I said. "Unless you'd rather ride in a Danford patrol wagon."

She started to walk to the corner. I was one step behind her, watching so that she would not dart away. I looked around at doorways and at standing people. Then I noticed a black sedan parked across the street. The car showed no lights. There was one man in the front seat, two in the rear. The car had a broken window held together with adhesive tape, and I knew it was Al Yekiti's.

"Get back," I shouted to her. I tried to jump in front of her to mask her body with my own. But I was not nearly fast enough.

There was a shock of flame from the sedan and six rapid shots. I scrabbled for my gun, twisting in the darkness, bringing it out from the hip holster. I ran forward, over the curb, out into the street. I fired at the sedan. Behind me I heard Helen's high-pitched scream.

Now I could see the German machine pistol protruding from the window of the sedan. The machine pistol flashed, burped and rattled again. I felt a hard wrenching blow hit my left arm. It spun me halfway around, numbing the entire side of my body. I lost my balance and fell down in the gutter. The gun dropped from my hand. There was a haze in front of my eyes as I fished for it. I found it. My fingers clutched the butt.

I got to one knee, then the other. I stood up, my left arm useless and dangling, feeling a warm wetness in it, the pain throbbing through the entire length of it to my very fingertips. I tried to brush the film from my eyes. My throat was parched and arid and I wanted a drink of water very badly. I stumbled in the direction of the car. I lifted the revolver and fired once again, this time trying to squeeze off the shot with a semblance of accuracy. The black car raced its motor and roared away. It turned a corner on screaming tires.

There was a babble of shrill voices from every direction. I heard the trilling sound of a police whistle, then the high-pitched, keening sound of a siren. I was looking for Helen Toledo.

I found her. She was down on the sidewalk, limp and shapeless like a large, oversized rag doll, her handbag open, the contents scattered near her. Her big hat was crushed under her head. Wide-eyed whispering bystanders hovered over her. I pushed through them, my dripping arm hanging awkwardly by my side. I bent down and lifted her head. I saw the darkly spreading blot on her pink coat. The crimson smear around her mouth was not lipstick.

135

Her eyes were open. Her mouth was open, the face fixed, rigid, immobile. I eased her head down again. A uniformed Danford cop was prodding me hard with his gun barrel. I brought out my wallet and showed the state badge. Then I stood up because Helen Toledo was dead and there was nothing left to do for her.

My arm was beginning to pain me badly. The Danford cops were arriving, filtering through the crowd and clearing the street. A street sergeant came through, bawling orders. Police cars stopped with squealing brakes. More cops came, milling around. A uniformed lieutenant came up to me.

"You the trooper?" he asked.

"Yes," I said. I was suddenly giddy, weak and light-headed. I sagged into him. He held me up, peered forward and saw my bloody sleeve.

"You've been hit," he said. He ripped my coat sleeve to the shoulder. "How bad is it?"

"I don't know," I said vaguely. "I can't move it."

He was tearing my shirt sleeve. The entire forearm was covered with blood. He took out a handkerchief and began to tie a tourniquet above the elbow. I winced.

"We'll get you to the hospital," he said, waving for the street sergeant.

"Wait a minute," I said hoarsely. "It was three men in a black sedan. Al Yekiti and two others." I gave him the registration number. "Call my barracks and have them get out roadblocks."

"Sure," the lieutenant said. "Sure. They won't get far."

CHAPTER 14 _____

THEY had me in a private room at the Danford General Hospital. I was sitting in a chair near the screened open window. My left arm was on a board splint, bandaged to the fingertips, and carried in a shoulder sling. I was wearing a striped cotton hospital robe. I stood up and began pacing the floor again as I had done this entire Sunday morning. I stopped at the window. Outside, on the hospital lawn, two aged patients sat in wheel chairs in the bright sun, heatedly discussing the Boston Red Sox.

Now I heard footsteps in the hallway. I turned around. Coming into the room was my father in his wheel chair, my mother behind it, pushing. My mother released the chair and came up to me a little breathlessly. I bent to kiss her.

"How do you feel, Ralph?" she asked worriedly. "Do you have pain?"

"No, I'm fine, Ma," I said. "Just a little throbbing."

"You look pale and thin," my father said. "You lost some blood, didn't you?"

"I'm all right now," I said. "They operated on me last night. They used a nerve block and froze the arm. It was a clean wound. The bullet tore a muscle and caused a few bone splinters. They sewed me up nicely. I'll be leaving here tomorrow."

"What kind of bullet was it?" my father asked.

"A nine-millimeter. It came from a Schmeisser machine pistol."

"Those hoods got clean away, didn't they?"

"So far, yes."

"You think I care about any gangsters?" my mother said. "Look at him, Walter, the boy's as thin as a rail. They probably don't feed him here. It's good I brought him some of my own chicken broth and calves' foot jelly. If I had him home, in one week I could—"

"Millie," my father said softly. "I want to talk to Ralph alone. You understand—"

Her eyes were moist. "Yes," she said. "I'll go speak to his doctor. Make the boy sit down in his chair."

She went out. My father wheeled over to the window. His face was haggard, the lines in it deeper than ever before.

"So," he said heavily, "it looks like I've caused all this. I started it. I let Ellen come to Danford."

"It happened," I said. "How were you to know?"

"I spoke to the Levesques," he said thinly. "I offered anything. I spoke to the Commissioner at GHQ. I called the D. A. here. What could they do for me, Ralph? They said the evidence—"

"Don't believe all the evidence," I said. "We're working on it. There are some new angles—"

138

He wasn't listening to me. He said, "It was my own damn interference. I've been like a kid playing with tin soldiers. If I had enough sense I would have known I was through with the troops since 1939. But no. Every time you came home I made you repeat everything you did. I was trying to feed memories, that's all." He looked up. "Do you like this life, Ralph? I never asked you before."

"I like it," I said.

"You might have finished college and become a chemist. This wouldn't have happened."

"No, I like this life, Pa," I said. "Remember the exams I took to get in? There were twenty-three hundred applicants and only fifty vacancies. I was scared I couldn't make it."

"Because of me?"

"Because I wanted to do it," I said. "Then when I was accepted into the training school I was scared I couldn't make the grade. Then when I graduated, you came to the exercises in your wheel chair. You sat up on the platform with the Governor and Major Carradine and the Commissioner. Seeing you there took away any doubts I had."

"I guess it was a proud day for me," he said. "I kept wiping my eyes. Maybe because when a man sits in a wheel chair all day, he thinks too much. Things are more emotional to him. He's got no way of letting off steam by physical action. But all the time I worry if I've done right."

"You've done fine by me, Pa," I said.

"You'll make a good trooper," he said quietly. "I know you've got the instinct for it." He took a deep breath. "We'll have to do something about Ellen. When you see a kid like Ellen grow up next door to you, and she's in your house all the time, she's like your own daughter."

"We'll get her out," I said.

"Does she mean enough to you? I mean, there's no more foolishness about it, is there?"

"No," I said. "I'm cured. And I'll get her out. I don't know how yet, but I'll get her out."

My father smiled wanly. "I come here to cheer you, and it's the other way around. Let's go find your mother before she tells the doctor how the hospital is starving you."

Detective-Lieutenant Ed Newpole came in the next day, Monday. I was in my own clothes then and getting ready to leave.

"They said you were being discharged," Newpole said. "But I thought it was later this afternoon."

"My arm's much better. I've got a small splint and bandage above the wrist. Look, I can move my fingers good."

"Great. Now you can go home and rest a few days."

"No, I want to go back to duty."

"When?"

"Now, Lieutenant. Right now."

Newpole took off his battered hat and scratched his head. "Well, I don't know if you're fit yet—"

"The surgeon-general was here this morning. He said I was able to do light duty. I'm fit. And there are three gunmen on the loose."

He looked amused. "You're not going to get them yourself, are you? And where are you going to find them?"

"They must be holed up somewhere."

"Sure. If they got through our roadblocks, they could be in hiding anywhere from Bangor, Maine, to Baltimore. That's going to take time."

"But we can't take the time," I said impatiently. "The longer it takes, the weaker the evidence."

"I don't understand," Newpole said. "What evidence? You were an eyewitness to Helen Toledo's death. You saw her get killed. What more do we need?"

"I'm talking about the evidence on Manette Venus. Captain Walsh has it."

"He has what?"

"The report of the conversation I had with Helen Toledo. Why do you think I was bringing Helen in? Why do you think they killed her?"

"You tell me," Newpole said.

"Because they knew she would have talked."

"All right," Newpole said. "And how can we check your story?"

I started to choke up. "If you think I lied—"

"Not me."

"Captain Walsh—" I said.

"No. He'd back up any statement one of his troopers made."

"Then what?"

"How's the D. A. going to take it, son? Where's the evidence? Here's a trooper whose girl is in the stir. He's in love with her. And don't tell me he's not. Because it shows on him like a heat rash. He's apt to try anything to get her out. With Helen Toledo dead, there's no corroboration."

"There's my word—"

"Not enough. The D. A. wouldn't listen to you and I don't blame him. I wouldn't either, if I were him."

"Listen," I said urgently. "They were getting ready to kill Manette Venus that night. They were there. In the house. Ellen Levesque walked into it. Some way, somehow, they saw an opportunity to pin it on her."

"It may be," Newpole said. "We've been thinking along

the same lines, too. But how was it done? Chet Granger and I have talked to Ellen over and over again. She fired the shot. There's no getting away from it."

"Let me talk to her," I said. "Let me see her."

"Why, sure," he said. "I got a hunch she wants to see you, too. She heard you were hurt."

"When can we go?"

"Now." He smiled. "Come on, I'll drive you over there. And I'll wait outside, too, so you can see her alone."

We drove to the county jail, to the women's section. They brought Ellen Levesque into the visiting room and sat her down in a straight wooden chair. There was a grayness about her. Her lips were pale and devoid of lipstick. It seemed as though the pigmentation of her skin had changed, but it was only the dreariness of the room.

"They told me you were shot," she said, her hand clutching my good one across the little table. "I was worried."

"I'm all right," I said. I wiggled the fingers of my left hand. "You can see for yourself."

She smiled briefly then. She turned her head and looked at the matron standing close by. "They don't give you any privacy, Ralph. It's very hard living in a goldfish bowl."

"I found out something in the Army," I said. "The trick is to make believe everybody else is invisible. I brought you some books, candy and cigarettes. I didn't know what else to bring. I had to leave them with the turnkey. If there's anything else you want—"

"Thank you. I have everything. Even a little radio."

"You look very good," I lied.

"Thanks, Ralph. Even if it isn't true. How's your father?"

142

"He's aged a little in the past week. He blames himself, naturally."

"He shouldn't. It wasn't his fault."

"It was my fault," I said. "Getting involved with Manette Venus the way I did. I keep thinking. If I went away with her, I wouldn't have messed it up for you, for everybody."

"Then you would have ruined your own life, Ralph."

"I don't know," I said.

Her voice chilled suddenly. "You don't know?" she asked distantly. "Don't you realize the kind of person she was? She was bad. All these things that have come out about her—"

"She wasn't bad," I said. "I don't care what they found out. I know she wasn't bad."

"But how can you reconcile such reasoning? Her record, her past—"

"I *know* she wasn't bad," I said stubbornly. "I don't know how to explain it—"

"One of your hunches. Your fabulous instinct."

"No. There's something wrong with the picture they have of her. Inside I have a feeling she was good and decent." I shook my head. "But that's gone and over with." I took her cold little hand. "Ellen, let's get married right away. It could be arranged here."

She looked at me intently. "You're not serious, are you?"

"Yes," I said. "They must have a chapel here where they can perform the ceremony."

"And why do you want to do it, Ralph?" she asked, her nostrils pinched. "Is this the grand, noble gesture?"

"No. I always wanted to marry you. Maybe at one time I didn't know it. But I do now."

"And do you think I would get married in a prison?" she

143

asked. "I always dreamed of getting married in the church in Cambridge. In a white satin dress and veil. With brides-maids and ushers and a flower girl. And what makes you think I would have you now?"

"I didn't consider that," I said slowly. "If I made one bad mistake—"

"Not one mistake, Ralph. Oh, a man can have a lapse. He can go sour just one time and get involved with a girl. And when you walked in here today I had already forgiven you. But now I know you're not honest. You won't admit you're wrong. You won't admit she was a bad girl. No, it would show your judgment is faulty and you can't have that, can you?"

"If I admitted she was bad," I said tonelessly, "I'd be lying to you."

"So now you're willing to perform the great act of charity. You're noble. You're going to do right by poor Ellen. You're willing to marry her. Do you think I could accept it?"

"You're bitter," I said. "It's this place. Once you get out of here you'll think differently."

"I won't," she said, her mouth tight. "And what makes you think I'll ever get out of here?"

"Because I think we've found something."

"Lieutenant Newpole told me. But he said it was very weak."

"It's a start," I said. "It gives us something to work on. If we could find these three men and question them—"

"But I fired the shot," she said in a dead voice.

"It's not right," I said. "Tell me about it again. From the beginning. Every step of the way."

"I've gone over and over it," she said dully. "I don't know

how many times I repeated it to how many assistant district attorneys and cops."

"Once more," I said urgently. "I'll help you with it. You came to the Reece house a little before seven-thirty. The cab driver let you off. He drove away?"

"Yes. He was an old, gray-haired man. He turned around and drove away. I saw the cab disappear."

"Were there any cars parked in the area? In the driveway? Along the side of the road?"

"I didn't see any," she said listlessly. "It was a bad night. The visibility was poor."

"You rang the bell," I said. "There was no answer. How long did you wait?"

"A moment. It was cold and drizzly. I was getting wet. I banged on the door then. I tried the knob. The door was unlocked."

"So you went inside. There was a light in the living room. Did you look around?"

"Yes. I didn't see anybody."

"Then you heard a radio upstairs."

"Yes."

"Music?"

"No, some announcer."

"Could you hear what he was saying?"

"No, his voice was indistinct."

"So you walked upstairs. You saw a light coming from under a door. You knocked. The voice stopped. How do you know it was really the radio?"

"What else could it have been? It wasn't Manette Venus."

"It could have been a man," I said. "He was inside the room with Manette Venus."

145

"But Manette opened the door when I knocked. There was nobody else in the room."

"She didn't open the door immediately," I said. "She asked who it was. There was a closet there. The man had a chance to hop inside."

Ellen thought for a moment. "It's possible, isn't it?"

"Yes," I said. "So Manette opened the door and let you in. There was an argument. She asked you to leave. She went to the dressing table and got a gun. *Where* was the gun?"

"In a drawer."

"So she brought the gun out. You moved forward and grabbed it. Where?"

"By the barrel. I twisted it away from her. Then I was holding it by the butt. I had my finger inside the trigger guard."

"But you were struggling with her," I said rapidly. "You swung around with your back to the closet door. You slipped. Something hit you on the back of the head. You lost consciousness. When you awoke, you were lying on the floor with the gun in your hand. One shot had been fired. Manette was lying dead with a single bullet through her. So you thought you did it. But you didn't. Instead, the man had come out of the closet. He hit you on the head, took the gun from your hand and shot Manette."

She looked at me for a long time. "It's no use," she said, shaking her head slowly. "*I* fired the gun. I remember it. I heard it. I saw the explosion. I felt the gun buck in my hand. It was *afterwards* that I swung around and struck my head."

I didn't know what to say then. The matron moved over

146

to us. "Something's wrong," I said hurriedly. "I know you didn't do it. You *couldn't* have done it."

She stood up. "Thanks," she said. "I have to go back now."

I reached out and grabbed her. I kissed her. Hard. There was no response. She was limp in my arms. She stepped back. Her eyes were lusterless. "It's no use, Ralph," she whispered. "You get an A for effort. Nothing more."

CHAPTER 15 _____

I went out with Ed Newpole the same afternoon. We met Captain Angsman of the Danford Police and Chet Granger, who had come back from Boston. We made the weary, tiresome rounds of saloons, poolrooms and flophouses. We questioned dozens of people. We found out nothing about Al Yekiti.

"He's not in Danford," Angsman said. "If he was, we'd have found his car."

"He could have dumped it and sneaked back," Newpole said.

"He's not in Danford," Angsman said.

In the evening Newpole and I were at Troop E Headquarters watching the out-of-state teletype reports come in. There was nothing on Yekiti yet. Newpole, his hat on the back of his head, moved back and forth along the bank of teletype machines, looking at one, then another. I leaned against the wall. My arm was aching quite badly and I was holding it up to slow the circulation a little.

I was about to go upstairs to my room to get some aspirin when Stan Maleski, the duty sergeant, poked his head into the communications room. He said, "Phone call for Lieutenant Newpole."

Newpole went out to the duty office. When he came back, he said to me, "It was Chet Granger. He's latched onto something. You want to go?"

"I'll get my hat," I said.

We hurried out of the barracks and into the black headquarters sedan. Newpole said, "Granger called from a public paybooth at Conti's. He trailed Fulton Reece there. Reece came with the same blond girl. And she's not his granddaughter, either."

It was on the turnpike, five miles outside of Danford. A long, low-slung wooden frame building with blue-shuttered picture windows in front. There was a large parking area. There was also a yellow neon sign that said *Conti's* in script lettering.

Inside, to the right of the checkroom, there was a small foyer. To the left there was a long narrow room which was the bar. There was a warm pungent odor of hickory smoke. The main dining room was softly lighted. It held rows of square, white-clothed tables. The room was almost completely filled with diners. In the center was a large brick grill. In front of it a cook, wearing a tall chef's hat, was barbecuing steaks over an open charcoal fire.

The headwaiter came up and spoke to Newpole. Newpole whispered something to him. The headwaiter smiled politely and moved away. In the main dining room, the chef flipped a steak high into the air, catching it deftly as it came down.

Lieutenant Granger came out of the bar. He met us in a corner of the foyer.

"Where are they?" Newpole asked him.

Granger moved his head imperceptibly. "On the main floor," he said. "Three tables to the left of the grill."

I looked. I saw Fulton Reece seated there. Next to him was an eighteen-year-old girl in a gold lamé dress. Her ash-blond hair was cut short and slicked to her head. Beside their table was a bucket stand with a bottle of wine in it.

"The man lives well," Newpole said. "He can't do it by taking in boarders. Who's the girl, Chet? Did you find out?"

Granger chewed on his gum. "Her name is Dolly Pine. She's on the habit. Heroin."

Newpole's mouth tightened. "She's pretty young to be on the habit."

"She's not only an addict," Granger said. "She's also on record for passing drugs."

"But she's only a baby," I said.

"Some start kind of young," Granger commented. "The Danford cops have a long record on her."

"How long has she been with Reece tonight?" Newpole asked.

"Since nine. He picked her up in his car. She was waiting on a Danford street corner for him. They drove here. They hung around the bar for a half-hour."

"They served her liquor here?"

"No. Miss Pine didn't have anything to drink."

"We'll have to take them in," Newpole said heavily. "Chet, you wait here for us."

150

He motioned to me and we went across the floor of the main dining room. We threaded through the tables and stopped in front of Fulton Reece. He looked up, startled. The girl stared at me with cold little eyes. She smoothed her dress at the waist and moved a pink tongue along her lips. She had a round, angelic, innocent face.

Reece lumbered to his feet, his face waxen. The pupils of his eyes were tiny, dreamy, half-closed. "Evening, Lieutenant Newpole," he said, slurring his words a little. "Hello, Lindsey. You here for a steak? Best steak house within fifty miles. Oh, but wait a minute. This is Miss Pine, daughter of a business associate of mine. Her father is going to join us later. Dolly, this is Detective-Lieutenant Newpole and Patrolman Lindsey of the State Police."

Dolly Pine smiled at us. Newpole said, "If you've finished your steak, Mr. Reece, I'd like you to—"

Reece interrupted feverishly. "What happened to your arm, Lindsey? There's a bandage showing under your sleeve. Oh, wait, don't tell me. I remember now reading about it in the papers. You were in a shooting scrap with that Yekiti hoodlum. Sit down and have a drink with us. Both of you."

"No, thanks," Newpole said quietly. "We'd like you to come with us, Mr. Reece. There are some questions we want to ask you at the barracks."

"What kind of questions?"

"If you'll step outside, please, we'll tell you."

"I can't leave Miss Pine. Her father—"

"We'll take Miss Pine, too."

"You'll what?" Reece asked with false belligerency. "See here, Lieutenant, you can't take this young girl along. Who do you think you are?"

"We know all about Miss Pine," Newpole said.

"Know what? Don't talk gibberish."

"The Danford Police have a record on Dolly since she was sixteen," Newpole said evenly. "Now, Mr. Reece, if you're ready—"

"I'll pay the check," Reece whispered. He looked wildly for the waiter. Then he threw some bills on the table. The waiter came over and started to say something.

"Take it all," Reece said hurriedly, with a quick gesture of his hand. "Take it all."

Dolly Pine stood up, her manner indifferent, her face an inanimate mask, her thin lips firm and unconcerned. She walked ahead of us, her small round hips moving rhythmically. Reece followed. Newpole and I brought up the rear.

In the foyer we were met by Granger. Reece said, "I have my car here."

"You can drive it to the barracks," Newpole said. "Lieutenant Granger here will go with you. Dolly will ride with Lindsey and myself."

We went out into the cool night air. In the dark parking lot, Newpole said, "Will you hold up your arms, Mr. Reece?"

Reece put his arms up high and Granger moved in and patted his clothes. From the inside breast pocket of the coat, Granger took out a long white envelope. He opened the flap. Inside were a dozen small envelopes. Granger opened one, dipped a finger inside and put the finger to his tongue. "Heroin," he said metallically.

Newpole turned to Dolly Pine. He said, "Would you open your handbag for us, Dolly?"

She giggled. "You think I carry a gun or something?"

"Worse than a gun," Newpole said seriously. "Let's have a look."

She giggled again. She opened her handbag. Newpole took out his pencil flashlight and shined it inside the bag.

"You carry quite a stock," he said.

"Business is good," she said.

Newpole put his hand out for the bag. She gave it to him. He went over to his sedan and opened the rear door. Dolly Pine picked up her skirt and stepped in. I got in front with Newpole.

We drove out of the parking area, Reece and Granger behind us. I turned and watched Dolly Pine. She sat in a corner of the rear seat, her fingers scrabbling on the up-holstery. She looked up and saw me watching her. She giggled inanely.

CHAPTER 16 _____

WE were in the guardroom of the barracks. In a corner sat a tall, angular state policewoman. In the center of the room, in a large chair, sat Dolly Pine. Her young face was smooth and emotionless. Captain Walsh was standing near the window rolling a cigar between his fingers. Granger stood near him, his jaw moving slowly over his gum. Newpole was walking back and forth in front of the big chair asking questions. He faced Dolly Pine and said, "And how long have you known Mr. Reece?"

"Oh, a couple of months," Dolly said.

Newpole brought out a picture of Manette Venus. "Did you ever see this girl?"

"Uh-uh."

"But you've heard of her."

She bobbed her head. "Sure, I heard of her. Fultie—I mean, Mr. Reece—he mentioned her."

"How?"

"She lived in his house. She was murdered there."

"Is that all he said about her?"

"He said she was pretty—the way I am. But he didn't like her."

"*Why* didn't he like her?"

She wrinkled her snub little nose. "He didn't want her around the house. But his old lady wanted a boarder and he couldn't say no to her."

"You think he and Manette had any trouble? Maybe he was mixed up in some deal and she found out about it."

She shrugged her shoulders. "Could be. He wanted her out."

"Or maybe they were in the deal together and they had a fight about it."

"I don't know if Fultie would fight with her. Fultie's a gentleman."

"He could have hired somebody else to get rid of her."

"Fultie? I don't know. The old boy's a soft one. He wouldn't do nothing himself. I know that."

Newpole rubbed his jaw. "Where were you last Thursday night?"

"That the night Manette got knocked off?"

"That's right."

She shook her head. "I don't know. I don't remember. I was out somewhere."

"Did you ever own a gun, Dolly?"

"What would I want with a gun?"

"Did you ever hear of Al Yekiti?"

"Sure, the papers have been full of him, the big bum."

"You know him well?"

"Him? That broken-down tramp? Naw. He never had

155

two nickels to rub together. Too cheap to get on the habit. Once I sold him a deck of weed."

"Marijuana?"

"Sure. What did you think I meant?"

"Did Fulton Reece know Yekiti?"

"I don't know. Fultie never mentioned him."

"You know Calvaris and Horace?"

"Uh-uh. But I heard of them. Smalltime stick-up artists."

"You haven't seen any of them around the past few days, have you?"

"Not since they knocked off Helen Toledo."

"You knew Helen?"

"Naw. I seen her working in the Starlight once."

Newpole took out his pipe and filled it slowly and methodically. He lit it and puffed on it for a moment. "How long have you been selling drugs to Fulton Reece?"

"I told you before," she said. "A couple of months."

"How did he contact you? How did he know you were a drug pusher?"

She looked down at the floor with a half-smile on her face. She didn't answer.

Newpole said, "What was the idea of the celebration at Conti's tonight?"

"Oh, Fultie was complaining the price was too high. He figured he'd romance me this way. He was only kidding himself with the big business tactics. I'd eat the steak but he'd still pay the price."

"Where do you pick up your drugs, Dolly?"

"Oh, here and there."

"Where?"

She smiled up at him. "You shouldn't ask. It's naughty to ask."

156

"Tell us, Dolly."

"Uh-uh. You should know better."

"We've notified Treasury. They'll be coming down to talk to you."

"It won't do the Feds no good."

Newpole puffed on his pipe. "You've got quite a load of dope in you now, Dolly. When it wears off you won't be feeling so good. I think you'll be talking then."

"I'll worry then, Lieutenant."

"You're charged with possession and sale of narcotics, Dolly. It's a big rap."

"I'll worry when the time comes."

"We've put a high bail on you. Ten thousand. Can you raise it?"

"Not now, I can't."

"Then the policewoman will have to take you down to the woman's detention in Danford. She'll take you into the dining room first and get you a cup of coffee."

"Gee, thanks," Dolly Pine said. She stood up and patted her hair. "You guys are real gentlemen. You give service."

They brought Fulton Reece in, his suit wrinkled, his tie askew. Newpole said, "Sit down, please, Mr. Reece, and take off your coat."

Reece took off his coat and sat down heavily. Newpole said, "Let me see your arm, Mr. Reece." He pulled up the sleeve of Reece's shirt. The veins from the elbow to wrist were discolored and purple. There were needle marks. The back of the hand was puffed.

There were beads of sweat on Reece's forehead. He said, "What did the girl tell you, Lieutenant?"

"Everything, Mr. Reece."

"A very stupid child," Reece said, without emotion, his voice tired in defeat. "I don't know what possessed me to take up with her."

"Drugs," Newpole said. "If not her, it would have been someone else."

"I'm entirely at your mercy," Reece said tonelessly. His mouth quivered and his jaw went slack. "Entirely. The Reece name, everything, is entirely at your mercy."

"Would you want another cup of coffee, Mr. Reece?"

"Thank you. But the sergeant gave me some in the dining room. I could use a white powder, of course. Just a small amount. A tiny bit of it would be sufficient."

"No, I'm sorry," Newpole said.

"If the girl told you everything, then what do you—?"

"Not about drugs," Newpole said. "We're interested in you and Manette Venus."

"I had nothing to do with her murder. I swear it."

"She was killed in your house."

"You think I—?" Reece shook his head. "But I didn't, Lieutenant. I didn't kill her. I was out with my wife that evening. I can prove we were at dinner at the Pioneer Club when Manette was killed. We came home and found her dead. We saw somebody run away."

"You had some kind of motive," Newpole said. "You didn't want Manette in the house. She found out you were taking drugs, didn't she?"

"Yes. But I wouldn't kill her because of it." The drug was wearing off in him. He began to yawn spasmodically. "You're making me sound like a hardened criminal. I'm not. I would never harm a living creature."

"You killed a Shetland pony when you were ten years old," Newpole said. "With a butcher knife."

158

"Oh, my Lord," Reece said, saliva appearing at the edge of his mouth. "To go back all those years. It was more than fifty years ago. I don't know how you found out. But to go back that far to besmirch me as a criminal isn't fair. I was a mere willful child then."

"Sometimes the roots go deep," Newpole said. "You're a sick man, Mr. Reece. Manette found out you were using drugs. You were afraid she might tell your wife, or the Danford Police. You might have hired somebody to kill Manette. Somebody like Al Yekiti, for example."

Reece looked around frantically at the impassive faces surrounding him. "I never met any Al Yekiti. I know he's a gangster who murdered a girl a few days ago. He shot this trooper here. I saw it in the newspaper. I never knew him."

"But you knew the girl he murdered. Her name was Helen Toledo."

"Yes," Reece said. He was yawning constantly now. "She came to the house once or twice to visit Miss Venus. I saw her at the Starlight Café twice afterwards."

"What were you doing there?"

"I was desperate." His head began to loll and saliva dripped from his chin. "Dolly was charging me enormous prices for heroin. I tried to make another contact. Helen Toledo looked like she was in the proper element to do something for me. I gave her twenty-five dollars."

"And what did she do?"

"Nothing," he said jerkily. "She kept delaying it, promising. I never got my money back, either, and there was nothing I could do."

"Everybody took a whack at you," Newpole said softly.

"I was desperate, sir."

"You need help, Mr. Reece."

159

"What can anybody do for me?"

"There's the federal hospital in Lexington, Kentucky. Arrangements can be made."

"But what can you do for me now, sir?"

"We have to book you for possession, Mr. Reece. But the bail will be only five hundred dollars."

"My wife is ill. The shock of it—the scandal—would be very grave."

"I'm sorry," Newpole said. "We have to go after the Dolly Pines and the big ones behind her. Through you we can do it. If you'll have somebody go bail for you, I'll call the bail commissioner now. After your bail is arranged you go home."

"I can't call anybody. I can't *tell* anybody."

"You have a family lawyer. That's what he's for."

"Very well," Reece whispered. "I'll give you his name. Please call him for me. It makes no difference anyway. Everything is over."

CHAPTER 17 _____

I was shaving in my hotel room, the next morning, Tuesday. Ed Newpole came in.

"How's the arm this morning?" he asked.

"Much better, thanks," I said. "It's improving every day."

"Good," he said. "I got a call from GHQ that the lab report on the Venus case is ready. Do you want to drive into Boston with me?"

I dropped the razor and began to wash off the lather. "When can we go?"

"Now," he said. "You're in a hurry, aren't you?"

"Like I've never been before."

"Sure, kid," he said. "But don't expect miracles. And let's stop for coffee first."

We drove along the wide, sinuous concrete ribbon that led to Boston. Newpole lit his pipe and puffed on it. He said, "Where's your pipe?"

"I'm afraid I'll chew the stem to bits," I said.

"No sense thinking too much about it," he said succinctly. "That way you're never too badly disappointed."

"I've had the breaks," I said. "It's not every boot trooper who gets a plain-clothes assignment like this. I'm grateful for it."

"Well, like I told you before, you knew the deceased and the suspect. We've done it in the past." He puffed methodically on his pipe. "Besides, I got a feeling in here for your old man. I was with him when he got shot. I suppose you knew that."

"Yes," I said.

"I've never forgotten it," Newpole said. "Not for a minute. It was my patrol out there that day. I was alone in my cruiser. I got the radio call to bring in that wife-beater. You know the rule, son. To bring in one man, you need only one trooper. And if a trooper can't bring in a man by himself, he can throw his badge on the desk." His pipe went out. He lit it again. "But your old man knew this wife-beater. He might duck out the back way when he saw me coming, and we'd be chasing him all over the woods. So this time your old man radioed me to come back to the barracks and pick him up. We'd both go. So we went out of there together. Your old man, being corporal and senior in command, took the front door. He didn't have to. He could have gone around the rear and sent me to the front. So your old man walked in and got shot in the back. It could have been me."

"You shouldn't think of it that way," I said. "My father never once said anything of the kind."

"No, he wouldn't. Not *your* old man. But I can't help thinking of it. I think of it all the time. And maybe that's

162

why I haven't seen him too much lately. When I do, I come home and feel like kicking the dog. You see, it might have been me in the wheel chair and your old man would be a troop commander or adjutant today."

"He never once complained," I said.

"No, he wouldn't. But I bet he thinks about it in the nights when he can't sleep. So I try to do the best I can. If I can give his kid a break, it's like giving him a break. I know what it means to him."

"Thanks," I said moodily. "I don't know if I've given him much help myself. He's been pretty sick over Ellen. If I hadn't started with Manette Venus—"

"Hindsight is always better than foresight," Newpole said. "Every man gets in trouble with a woman at least once in his life. Seems like a natural process almost, like getting bald. Sometimes the man is single, more often he's married. Most of the time it straightens out by itself and nobody is the wiser. When it does make trouble, it's always somebody else who takes the big rap for it. Funny how it works out. Seems it's always a wife, or sweetheart, or mother or father, or somebody in the family who suffers the most."

"Yes," I said. "And sometimes all of them."

We came through Worcester and along Route 9, past Framingham and the big red-brick buildings of Troop A Headquarters. Behind it were the Quonset huts of the training school where I had spent three months.

We came into the mushrooming suburbs of Boston—Natick, Wellesley, then Newton and Brookline. We turned off at Brookline Village and drove across to Commonwealth Avenue.

The Department of Public Safety was at 1010 Commonwealth Avenue. It was a large, square, factory-type building. The Ballistics Room of GHQ was on the fourth floor. There was a grilled steel entrance door which opened by electrical contact.

It was my first time there. Two of the walls were lined with glass cases displaying hundreds of pistols of all makes and calibers. In the corners were machine guns mounted on tripods. High on one wall were rifles, shotguns, foreign weapons, submachine guns, dirks, machetes, daggers, blackjacks and spring knives. There was a complete display of ammunition, carefully catalogued and labeled. In the rear were the filing cabinets and microscope tables. I recognized the square-mouthed centrifugal bullet catcher, and the wadding boxes used to retrieve bullets.

Sitting at his desk, wearing the uniform of a lieutenant in the State Police was Robert Clyde, Chief Ballistician. He was forty-eight years old, but his hair was prematurely gray, thin, and parted in the middle. He had a serious, stern-visaged face. Over his left eye there was a small clefted scar. Hovering in the rear of the room was S. O. Sergeant Philip Dexter, tall, young and light-haired.

I knew Lieutenant Clyde. He had come to the house several times and he had given a course in ballistics to us at the Training School. He stood up. He was tall and well-built. He reached out and shook hands with me, smiling diffidently. "Hello, Ralph. I just saw your father a few days ago."

"I guess he didn't look so good, sir," I said.

"We're all getting old," Clyde said. "You've met Phil Dexter, haven't you?"

"I've seen him at the Training School," I said. I shook hands with Dexter and he went back to his microscope table.

"Sit down," Clyde said. He pursed his lips. "Ed, it's an interesting case Chet Granger brought me."

"You mean you could do something with it?" Newpole said.

"A lot," Clyde said. I looked at his desk. On it was the .32-20 pearl-handled Colt revolver, a tag tied to the trigger guard. I rested my wounded arm on my knee and waited.

Clyde said, "The bullet Chet Granger brought was a .32-20 Colt cartridge. When it was fired, the bullet penetrated the head of the victim, Manette Venus. The copper jacket of the bullet separated from the lead core and remained in the brain. The rest of the bullet went through and imbedded itself in the south wall of the room. I matched up the copper fragments from the brain, with the core of the bullet from the wall. Danford Ballistics was right. It's from the same cartridge. There's no argument there. Not at all."

Clyde stood up and left his desk. He went over to a rear table. "Come here and look into this comparison microscope, Ed. On the left is a test bullet fired from the gun. On the right is a large copper fragment from Manette Venus' brain."

Newpole stepped over and peered into the eyepiece. He turned around slowly and there was a peculiar look on his face. He said, "Take a look, Ralph."

I went over and squinted into the microscope. "I see a bunch of lines and scratches."

"Those are the barrel lands and striations," Clyde said. "Look at both of them. Do they match?"

"It doesn't look that way to me, sir," I said.

"They don't match," Clyde said. The skin crinkled around his shrewd blue eyes. "The bullet that killed

Manette Venus didn't come from the gun in Ellen's hand."

I just stood there. Unconsciously I began to grope for cigarettes in my pocket with my wounded arm. I didn't know what I was doing and I didn't care. "Then someone else killed Manette Venus," I said inarticulately.

"So it seems," Clyde said. "The barrel lands on the copper show the murder gun was a six left. That means it was another .32-20 Colt or some Spanish imitation."

"Wait a minute," I said. "The other gun *was* a .32-20 Colt. Manette Venus' gun was a twin. She said there was a pair of them."

"So I remember you told me," Newpole said. "And it's one reason why I had this gun checked here. But Manette never told you where the other gun was."

"No," I said. "I guess I never asked her, either. But can't you see? There *was* a man in the closet. He had the other gun. While the girls were struggling, he opened the door, fired, and killed Manette. Then he struck Ellen on the head."

"I don't think so," Clyde said. "The pictures they sent me show a powder dispersion on Manette's forehead. The bullet wasn't fired more than six inches away. The way it could have happened was this. Maybe the girls fought for the gun. Ellen, at the time, was facing the window. The window was wide open, wasn't it? No trees or anything around?"

"The window was open," Newpole said. "And there are no trees around the house."

"So the bullet missed Manette," Clyde said. "It could have gone out the window. According to Ellen's statement they kept struggling for a few seconds longer. They were near the closet. The man in the closet opened the door and

166

hit Ellen on the head with the butt of his gun. Then he shot Manette with his own gun. That's all. He took off quick."

"He was there with the intention of killing Manette," I said.

Clyde smiled. "We don't know what his intentions were. We don't even know who the person is. I figure it's a man because Ellen heard a man's voice on her way up the stairs. Anyway, the man was holding the twin Colt, if there is one. He could have hidden in the closet. When he heard the girls struggling and the gun go off, he poked his head out. He saw Manette was still alive and here was his chance to finish the job. So he did. I don't know if he figured it then as a perfect crime or anything. But it pretty near turned out that way. Because the cops found Ellen with a .32-20 Colt in her hand, and she admitted firing the shot. The man could have been just plain lucky the way it happened. Seems to me it wasn't a planned job at all. Nobody knew Ellen was coming to Danford."

"If it wasn't for you, Lieutenant—" I started to say.

"Nothing stupendous about it," Clyde said. "Granger was able to bring the copper fragments here. And we were able to see if they matched a test bullet fired from the gun. They didn't."

"I don't know why I'm standing here like this," I said happily. "I've got to get back to Danford and get Ellen out of jail."

Clyde started to laugh. Newpole grinned. He said, "And how are you going to do that, boy?"

"Well, I'd go down and tell the D. A.—"

"It's a little more than that," Newpole said. "It has to go through channels. Bob Clyde will notify Granger that the ballistics evidence on Ellen Levesque has gone out the window. If that's all they have, they can no longer hold her on anything. Granger will go to the D. A. in Danford and explain it to him. Then the D. A. will most likely arrange for her immediate discharge."

Clyde nodded. "I'll get on it right away. But first, Ralph, you ought to phone your father, don't you think? Go ahead, use my phone."

"Yes, sir," I said.

I went for the telephone on Clyde's desk. Newpole took out his pipe and looked at it solemnly.

"Well," he said. "It's back to Danford again. There's still a murderer running around loose."

CHAPTER 18 _____

WE were driving back to Danford. Newpole was behind the wheel. We had passed the new Route 128 turnpike when Newpole looked over at me.

"For a happy guy," he said, "you're kind of quiet. You haven't said a word."

"I can smoke my pipe now," I said. I took it out and stuffed tobacco into it. "I've been doing some thinking, Lieutenant. It seems I've got a clearer mind now."

"That's the trouble with personal feelings," Newpole said. "It throws your mind out of gear. A cop has to look at everything in a detached way. Otherwise he's going to mistake sentiment for fact."

"I've been thinking of Al Yekiti," I said. "He could have been the man in the closet."

"I might buy that, too," Newpole said.

"Yekiti knows the territory around Danford," I said, putting a match to the bowl of my pipe. "He's pulled stick-ups in the area and gotten away for a little while. He could have gone around the roadblocks."

"We have a fifteen-state alarm out for him," Newpole mused. "He hasn't shown anywhere. And Yekiti is an easy man to identify. It could be somebody is hiding him out."

"Something else has been bothering me," I said. "It's like a daisy chain. Yekiti was friendly with Helen Toledo. Helen was friendly with Manette Venus. And Manette Venus worked in the office of the Staley Woolen Company. She had been there a month."

"If you're going to link chains, I can link myself to one of the kings of Ireland."

"I was thinking some more," I said. "My Friday morning patrol is the Staley Wool area. Just before noon there's a payroll delivery by armored car. The payroll is two hundred thousand dollars."

Newpole slowed the car. He stared over at me. "I didn't know that," he said softly. "I'll be damned if I knew it. Why didn't you mention it before, Ralph?"

"Because I didn't think of connecting it then," I said. "Now I can." But as I said it, the cockiness went out of me. I had been wrong in not remembering about the Friday patrol and I knew it. And if I had looked with smug tolerance at the plodding, painstaking methods of Newpole and Granger and Clyde, it was out of me now. Because they would have remembered, and they would have put the information in its proper niche.

Newpole said, "Did Manette Venus know about your patrol?"

"Yes."

"She knew the exact patrol route?"

"No, sir. I didn't tell her. Each week the route is changed.

Lieutenant, there's an old guard at the front gate. If a holdup was planned, the guard could be grabbed quick. Inside the gate is the office building. There the door is made of steel and it's locked from the inside, and they have another guard stationed behind it. So they couldn't use that way. But around the side there's a fire escape leading to the second floor. It's there where the money is counted and separated."

"Is the fire door kept locked?"

"Yes, from the inside. Manette Venus worked in that office. She could unlock the door. Yekiti and his gang could come up the fire escape, in through the door, grab the payroll and go out the same way."

Newpole stared fixedly at the road ahead. "But you would be cruising around outside. They would have to get you out of the way."

"Yes, sir," I said. "I come from a different direction each time and I'm always near the gate when the armored truck comes out."

Newpole nodded his head. "Manette Venus was damn curious about your weapons and patrols, wasn't she?"

"Yes, sir. She asked me a lot of questions."

"It might fit," Newpole said. "They could have done it in many ways. They could have put Manette on the road in a car. She'd have a flat tire or something. You'd come along. Naturally you'd stop. You'd talk. You might even help her with the tire. That would throw your schedule haywire. It would give Yekiti a chance to get away on another road. With good timing, the job could have been pulled."

"I'm sure of it."

171

"Never say sure," Newpole said. "It makes a good story. But so far it's only theory."

"A job like that takes planning," I said. "Yekiti must have had maps and weapons. If we could find them—"

"I say it's worth a shot," Newpole commented. "Let's go into Danford and scratch around."

We were bunched together in a small group in front of Yekiti's rooming house. Lieutenant Newpole and myself, Captain Angsman and two plain-clothes men from the Danford police.

"I'll try anything," Angsman said skeptically. "If you want to go in and have another look, it's okay with me. But I've had this place staked out ever since Yekiti took off."

We went inside. Newpole stood in the middle of Yekiti's littered room, his hands on his hips. His eyes scanned the slitted, gouged, overstuffed furniture.

"We searched all through this joint, "Angsman told him. "I don't think we missed anything, Ed."

"Well, once more won't do any harm," Newpole said. He went into the closet and tapped the wall for false partitions. He came out and started for the bathroom.

"We checked there," Angsman called to him. "I even had the plumbing trap opened. I had the flooring tapped for loose boards or new nails."

Newpole nodded absently. He dragged a chair to the windows. He stood on the seat, reached up and ran his fingers along the top molding. He came down and brushed his hands.

"All right," he said. "I guess there's nothing here." He looked at me pensively.

"Yekiti worked at Reach Forwarding Company," I said tentatively. "It's worth a try there, isn't it?"

The Reach Forwarding Company was a large building. It was built of corrugated steel and had large casement windows. It stood on a railroad siding. At the loading platform, men were dollying crated furniture onto a freight car. I stood on the platform and watched them. Then I turned around because the superintendent was speaking to Ed Newpole.

"I had a lot of patience with Yekiti," the superintendent was saying. "He was one of these hard characters and no good at all. He was lazy and always late. And half the time he'd show up with a jag on. But we're short of help. He had a strong back and I was able to get *some* work out of him."

"What shift did he work?" Newpole asked.

"Mostly on the night shift."

"How many days a week would he work?"

"Average, two or three. Depended on how much money he needed for liquor."

"Did he ever tangle with the other men here?"

"Plenty at first. He was a troublemaker. Liked to push people around. But one night they ganged up on him and fought back. After that he kept to himself."

I moved in closer. "Where did he eat his lunch, sir?" I asked.

The superintendent scratched his head. "He ate it here. He didn't go out."

Newpole looked at me, then at the superintendent. "Where in here?"

"Now I don't know. Back in a corner somewhere."

"By himself?"

"Yeah. Who was going to eat with him?"

"Maybe he wanted to eat alone for a reason," Newpole said. "Maybe he had something hidden in there. Can you find out where he ate?"

"I'll ask the men," the superintendent said.

He went away. Captain Angsman and a Danford detective joined us. The superintendent came back and motioned to us. We went into the cool dim interior of the building. We passed huge stacks of baled wool, cartons, crates of machinery. There was furniture wrapped in excelsior and brown kraft paper.

The superintendent stopped. "Here," he said. "This little bench in the corner. He'd sit here and eat his lunch."

I looked down and saw the small wooden bench. Behind the bench was a partition of boards. The boards came shoulder high. Above the boards, meshed chicken wire ran as high as the ceiling. There was an unpainted wooden door. It had a hasp and a brass padlock.

Newpole saw it, too. He said, "What's behind this door?"

"Damaged goods," the superintendent said. "Claim stuff. We store it there for the insurance adjusters."

"There's no use asking if Yekiti had a key?" Newpole said.

"Him?" the superintendent snorted. "No, sir. I've got the one key."

"It's only a padlock," Angsman said, examining it curiously. "It can be opened with a hairpin."

"Let's take a look inside," Newpole said.

The superintendent took out a long key chain. He fitted a key to the padlock. The door opened and we went in.

We found everything in a far corner of the room. There

174

was an empty, upended plywood packing carton. Under it were two battered suitcases. Newpole opened the first one.

Wrapped in oily, soiled canvas was a set of burglars' tools. There were a sawed-off shotgun, two Belgian nine-millimeter automatic pistols, and extra clips of ammunition. There was a large brown paper bag. In it were three grotesque Hallowe'en masks.

Newpole opened the other suitcase. There were six tall metal canisters. They were painted gray. The markings had been scraped off, showing slivers of shiny steel underneath. There was no .32-20 Colt revolver.

Angsman picked up one of the canisters and sniffed at it. He hefted it. "They look like Navy smoke bombs," he said.

Newpole took the bomb from him and examined it. "What do you think, Charlie? You think they were planning a job at Staley Woolen?"

Captain Angsman pushed back his natty hat. "I don't know, Ed," he said in a puzzled voice. "Yekiti never held up anything bigger than a grocery store or a gas station. He was a bum who could strong-arm a few small shopkeepers and that's all. Where would he get an idea as big as this?"

"Manette Venus could have fed it to him," Newpole said. "Also, he's been in and out of state prison. A man can pick up an education in there."

"Maybe," Angsman said. "I guess it was an important enough job to him. Otherwise he wouldn't have killed his own girl friend, Helen Toledo, to keep her from talking. Oh, he's a nice boy, our Al."

"For two hundred grand," the Danford detective said,

"Yekiti would kill his own mother. If he ever had one."

"We'll latch onto him," Angsman said. "He has to show somewhere. A torpedo like him can't hole up forever."

Newpole nodded his head. "Sure, he'll show. Soon he's going to need breathing room. In the meantime, we'll send these weapons to Bob Clyde. Maybe they've been used on other jobs."

We came outside. Angsman and his man drove off. Newpole got into his sedan and waited for me to get in beside him. He grinned at me. "Well, maybe you hit it on the nose, son. I don't know if it was good logic, instinct or plain luck. Or maybe all three. But I don't argue with success."

He started up the car and we bumped over the railroad tracks. He said, "We'll keep looking for Yekiti. Which means there's not much else for you to do, Ralph. We'll run a check on Fulton Reece and Dolly Pine. I've already sent to the Chicago cops for a tracer on the Fleers. And we've asked the New York cops to do a few chores." He smiled wryly. "So I guess that winds it up for you."

"I've had an education," I said.

"I'm glad," Newpole said. "You've got the makings of a good detective. In four years or so, you'll be eligible to take the exams for detective-lieutenant, won't you?"

"Yes," I said. "But I've got an idea I'll be staying in the uniformed branch."

"Sure," he said. "Sure. I kind of thought you'd keep it in the family."

CHAPTER 19 _____

THAT evening I was back in uniform. I had had my arm dressed and I was sitting in the barracks dining room having a cup of coffee with Captain Walsh.

Ed Newpole, who had been in the communications room, came in and poured himself a cup from the percolator. He said, "I phoned Reece and asked him to come by the barracks and have a talk with us."

"Now?" Walsh asked.

"Yes," Newpole said. "Reece is in tough shape, I guess. He's been acting so bad his attorney got him a continuance on the narcotics charge."

"I know it," Walsh said. "The Danford cops have a man watching him."

"Why?" Newpole asked.

"He might run," Walsh said.

"I'm afraid he's got no place to go," Newpole said.

"I'm not so sure," Walsh said.

Ray Beaupré, the duty sergeant, came into the dining room. "Got a call from the Danford cops," he said. "They lost Reece."

Walsh stood up. "Dammit," he said. "How?"

"They were tailing his car, Captain. They lost him in traffic. The last they saw he was heading west on the pike. Going fast."

Walsh said, "Get out a Signal Three to all cruisers in that sector. I want Reece picked up and brought in."

"Yes, sir," Beaupré said, running for the communications room.

Walsh turned to Newpole. "I thought you said Reece wouldn't run?"

"I've been wrong before, Fred."

"Here's another thing," Walsh said. "Reece was in debt. He needed money for drugs. Also, he was the one who installed the security setup at Staley Woolen, and he'd know how to break it down. There are a lot of questions we have to ask him about Manette Venus and Yekiti."

"Which is why I asked Reece to come in here," Newpole said wearily.

There was a silence in the dining room. Ten minutes went by. Walsh was picking up his coffee cup when suddenly he turned his head. From the communications room we could hear the short staccato bark of an incoming radio call. The communications man came running out of his room and into the duty sergeant's office.

We pushed our chairs back and hurried into the office.

Ray Beaupré looked up from his night lamp. "A smash-up," he said tersely. "Went off the highway ten miles west in Claxton. I'm putting in an ambulance and doctor call."

"What's the license number?" Newpole said.

178

Beaupré gave it. Newpole turned away, his face taut and inflexible. "It was Reece," he said to Walsh. "We'd better get out there, Ralph."

We raced down the turnpike in a patrol cruiser, siren screaming, red roof light flashing. I sat hunched forward over the wheel. Every time I swung the car around occasional traffic, my left arm stabbed with pain.

Ahead of us, at the bottom of a hill, we saw red flares on the road. I slowed the car. Now I could see the blinking red light of a cruiser on the shoulder of the highway. I stopped the car and we jumped out. There was a pall of smoke.

People milled around. We broke through them. The car was off the road, pushed into a thick-trunked, tall oak tree. The motor had splintered and disintegrated. The smashed front windshield lay against the trunk of the tree. The steel body of the car was crumpled like an accordion, the frame twisted and warped. There was a smell of scorched paint and the acrid odor of burnt rubber. A steady cloud of smoke and steam rose up.

At the left side of the car, Phil Kerrigan, his face blackened and the front of his uniform smudged, tugged at the twisted door with a jack handle. Another trooper, a short dark boy named Manny Green, was playing a hand fire extinguisher on the front of the car. I moved close and looked through the shattered glass of the side window. I saw Fulton Reece slumped over the steering wheel. Kerrigan strained on the jack handle and the door snapped open.

We dragged Fulton Reece out and laid him on the shoulder of the road. Kerrigan knelt down beside him. He pulled

179

out a flashlight and lifted the eyelids. Then he closed them. He stood up and shook his head slowly.

"Anyway," Newpole said, "it was a good try."

Green had been pushing the crowd back. Now he came over. "Dead?" he asked.

"As soon as he hit, I think," Kerrigan said. He bent down and wiped his hands on a tuft of tall brown grass. "I can't understand it, Lieutenant. It was a clear straightaway. A tire didn't go. It's almost like he turned off deliberately into the tree."

"Yes," Newpole said. "Now I think we'd better move everybody back. The gas tank is liable to go up."

There was the sound of a keening siren. It became louder and closer. It came down the hill and stopped with a low growl. I looked around and saw the ambulance. A white-coated doctor jumped out and ran over to us. He carried a black bag in his hand.

I reported to Captain Walsh's office the next morning. He was standing at the big wall map. He said, "The troop and all substations have searching patrols out in every direction." He turned away from the map and went back to his desk. "You've still got a bad arm, and I need a cruiser for traffic patrol."

"But I'm feeling fine, sir," I said. "I could—"

"You'll patrol the turnpike east of Danford. Ten miles. That's all."

"Yes, sir," I said. I put on my cap and went out.

The traffic was light and the patrol card showed only a small stolen car list. There was a haze in the fields and the sun was pale and the air crisp and sharp. I drove along slowly on the far right side of the road. Ahead of me I saw the junction of Route 105. I pulled over and stopped the cruiser.

It wasn't a hunch or instinct this time, but cold reasoning. I was putting myself in Al Yekiti's position and thinking what I would do if I were him. He wouldn't go back to Danford after the killing. The Danford cops would be shaking down every hiding place in town. He would head out. But if he headed out too far he would run into the State Police roadblocks. Perhaps he had gone around them. And perhaps he had not.

I decided to go off territory. I didn't cut off my radio but I didn't call in and tell them, either. I turned onto Route 105 toward Bellfield. I went by the same farmhouses of a week ago, the same rocky fields and the gnarled apple trees.

I came to the narrow dirt road which lead to Deer Pond. I turned the cruiser in, jouncing slowly over the ruts and rocks. A quarter of a mile before the pond I stopped in the middle of the road. I got out. I walked up the hill. I cut through the trees to the edge of the clearing. I stood behind a tall pine. Across the brown carpet of needles I could see the yellow Boothbay cottage. It was bleak and lifeless.

Beyond the cottage, the blue waters of Deer Pond sparkled in the October sun. There was no sign of human life. I went back to the road and continued on, following it as it wound around the pond. I searched the ground for tire tracks. I watched both sides of the road for telltale signs in the underbrush.

I walked five hundred yards, six hundred. Then I saw something. There were brush marks on the dirt road, as though somebody had swept there with branches. Then, on the right side, there were some matted broken weeds. They had been fluffed up, but the swath they had made was about the width of a car.

I turned off the road. I pushed into the underbrush, the brambles scratching against my puttees. I opened the flap of my holster and loosened the long-barreled revolver. My shoes crackled on the dry leaves. I followed the swath. I came upon some brown pine branches banked up high. I walked around them first. Then I moved in and began to pull them away. Hidden behind them was a car. It was Al Yekiti's black sedan.

I circled around the car, pulling away pine branches. There was a bullet hole through one side and another through one window. I opened the door and looked inside. It was musty-smelling and empty. The upholstery was stained and torn.

I left there. I went back to the road. I walked down, past the Boothbay cottage, to my cruiser. I radioed Troop E Headquarters. When I was through I left the cruiser and went back up the road again. I stood behind a tree at the edge of the clearing and kept watch on the cottage.

I didn't hear the cruisers coming. The only way I knew was that a fine haze of dust began to drift above the trees below me. I went down the road to meet them.

They had parked the cars among the trees. There were six men, including Captain Walsh, Sergeant Beaupré and Corporal Arthur Sherman. The corporal carried a tear-gas gun. Manny Green held a Winchester rifle. Kerrigan and Ravelli had shotguns crooked under their armpits.

"Did you see anybody in the cottage?" Walsh asked me.

"No, sir," I said. "But their car isn't far. If Manette Venus knew about the cottage, then Yekiti would know, too."

"You didn't show yourself, did you?"

"I don't think so, sir."

"I like my men eager, but not that eager." Walsh turned around. "Beaupré, we'll go up and reconnoiter. Lindsey, take a Thompson and come with us."

Kerrigan reached into a cruiser and handed me a sub-machine gun. I went up the dirt road with Walsh and Beaupré. We came off the road, crouched down and crawled through the dry-smelling underbrush. We stopped at the edge of the clearing. The wind sighed through the pines. The sun dappled the carpet of pine needles. A bird twittered somewhere. A squirrel ran up a tree and chattered at us from a high perch. A vagrant breeze rippled the waters of the pond.

Walsh studied the yellow cottage. "No sign of life," he said, out of the corner of his mouth. "No smoke coming from the chimney."

"If you want me to go take a look—" Beaupré said.

"No," Walsh said. "It's possible they're in there. If they had a supply of food stashed away, they wouldn't have to move for a while."

I spoke to him from my prone position. "I could go ahead and show myself, sir. Maybe I could draw their fire."

"You won't do anything of the kind," Walsh snapped. "Let's go back."

We crawled back to the road. We walked down and joined the others. Walsh glanced at their somber faces.

"We'll surround the cottage," he said in a measured voice. "You'll use cover. Make sure you have a good thick tree trunk in front of you. And nobody does anything until he gets the signal. Beaupré, you'll distribute your three men. Corporal Sherman and Lindsey, you keep with me."

The pale blue tunics and dark blue breeches spanned out and melted away in the woods. Walsh looked at the intent face of Sherman, then at me. He took out his pocket watch and held it in his hand. We waited silently. He put the watch away and walked up the road again. Sherman and I followed him.

"Wait here," Walsh said. He stepped forward into the edge of the clearing and showed himself.

"Yekiti!" he called. "Calvaris! Horace! You're surrounded. Come out with your hands up."

There was no answer from the cottage. The wind sighed through the trees again.

"Yekiti!" Walsh called out.

He waited for an answer. There was none. He came back to Sherman and me. His face was red from the shouting.

"Either they're not in there," he said, "or they're playing possum."

"I'll go take a look," Sherman said.

"Let's have no more of that," Walsh said quietly. "Lindsey, you cover me. I'm going down there."

He walked out. He started slowly for the cottage. He seemed small and forlorn out there by himself. I brought the Thompson up and wrapped the canvas thong tightly against my arm.

There was a tinkle of glass from the cottage. Three rapid pistol shots crackled in the still air. Walsh hit the ground face down. I fired a burst at the cottage with the Thompson. Then another. Walsh stood up and ran back, his short sturdy legs churning the ground.

"Lousy shots," he said, breathing heavily from behind his tree trunk. "And I'm no small target, either." He twisted his body around. "Okay, so they're in there." He cupped his

184

hands and shouted, "Sergeant Beaupré! Give them a shotgun blast."

A second passed. There was the explosion of a shotgun, then two together. Then a fusillade. The cottage windows shattered.

There was a rapid answering fire from the cottage. I could hear the distinctive burp of a German Schmeisser machine pistol. Now came the single shots of revolver fire and the high-powered whine of a repeating rifle. A faint smoke filtered through the cottage windows. Bullets thumped against tree trunks, or ricocheted and screamed away. Pine cones fell. Pine needles wafted down.

"I'd like to take them alive," Walsh said soberly. "I don't care about Yekiti. He wouldn't talk anyway. But if Calvaris and Horace are in there we could get information from them."

Sherman was putting a tear-gas shell into his gun. He tested for wind direction. "Maybe those two want to surrender, sir. But they're afraid of Yekiti."

"It's worse for them this way," Walsh commented. "All this will do is get them killed."

A bullet pinged off the tree in front of Walsh. He squeezed his thick body back. "That was close," he said. He nodded to Corporal Sherman. "Give them a whiff of tear gas, Arthur."

The corporal lifted the short, fat-barreled rifle and sighted it along a tree branch. He fired. The tear-gas shell arched through the air and hit the ground at the edge of the cottage. A gray cloud of smoke rose up.

"Another, Arthur," Walsh said. "Bring up your elevation."

Sherman fired again. The shell looped through the air,

bounced on a window sill and dropped inside the cottage.

"Lucky," Sherman grinned.

"Good," Walsh said grimly. "Another. And bring it up a fraction more."

Sherman pushed another shell into the chamber and fired again. The shell lobbed through the air and through the jagged glass of the window. Smoke billowed out.

Walsh turned to me. "You were in the cottage before, weren't you, Lindsey?"

"Yes, sir."

"Were those rooms fully enclosed?"

"No, sir. They were partitioned only as high as the eaves."

"Good," Walsh said. "They won't be able to shut off the room with the tear gas in it. It'll spread." He cupped his hands. "Beaupré! Hold your fire."

The firing died away. Among the trees there was a stillness. We waited. The smoke drifted away from the cottage. We could hear coughing from the troopers near the lake.

Suddenly the front door of the cottage opened and two men burst onto the porch. They were covering their eyes with their hands, but I recognized them as Calvaris and Horace. They felt around for the screened porch door, opened it and stumbled down the stairs. Tears ran down their faces.

"This way!" Walsh called. "Here!"

They turned in the direction of his voice. They staggered like blind, drunken men.

Now a huge figure loomed in the doorway of the cottage. Yekiti came onto the porch, with the machine pistol in his hands. He coughed. He began to scream loudly and obscenely at Calvaris and Horace.

"Drop the gun!" Walsh called to him.

Calvaris and Horace ran, zigzagging over the ground. Yekiti didn't drop the gun. He fired through the screening of the porch, spraying bullets at the two running men. I saw puffs of dust as Horace was hit. He fell down, rolled over and lay still. Calvaris screamed and dropped to the ground. He began to crawl on his stomach, his hands pulling at tree roots.

I broke into the clearing and aimed the Thompson at Yekiti. It jumped in my hands. The porch screening shredded. Yekiti dropped his machine pistol. He hit the screen door, tore it away from its hinges. He tumbled down the three steps to the ground.

Captain Walsh ran for him. I was close behind. At the porch stairs I looked down at Yekiti, not recognizing him now in the gore and filth, the face shattered beyond a semblance of humanity. Captain Walsh poked at the huge body with his toe.

"So that's the end of him," Walsh said. He pushed his revolver back into its flap holster. "If he'd have lived any longer, he'd have mangled a few more old shopkeepers." He turned to me. "How does it make you feel, Lindsey?"

"A little squeamish inside, sir. It's not like war. It's like hunting wild animals."

"It's a job we have to do sometimes. I never could stomach it myself. I won't be eating any more today."

"You sir?"

"Me. In all these years I've never gotten used to it."

The other troopers were now in the clearing. Phil Kerrigan was examining the dead body of Horace. Sergeant Beaupré was putting handcuffs on Dick Calvaris. Calvaris was crying hysterically. Walsh heard the crying.

"Beaupré," he said. "Maybe you'd better check and see if he was hit somewhere."

"Not a scratch on him," Beaupré said. "Calvaris is scared, that's all."

Walsh went up the stairs, through the porch and into the cottage. I followed him. The remains of the tear gas made me cough and sputter. My eyes smarted and tears gushed out of them. Walsh kept dabbing his eyes with a handkerchief.

There was a shambles of crockery. There were scattered, opened cans of food and rinds of fruit. Empty whisky bottles and empty beer cans. A litter of cigarette butts. They weren't even animals, I thought. Animals would have lived there cleaner.

The pine walls were pockmarked with bullet holes. My shoes crunched on broken glass. There were a .30-30 Winchester rifle and a .45 Colt automatic pistol.

Corporal Sherman came in with Manny Green and Hank Ravelli. They searched the cottage systematically, from one end to the other. There was no .32-20 Colt.

I heard footsteps on the porch. Phil Kerrigan came in. Behind him was the slim form of Cole Boothbay. Boothbay walked up to Captain Walsh.

"You phoned me from the barracks earlier," Boothbay said. "You said something about criminals living here. Was that it?"

"That was it," Walsh said.

Boothbay stopped short and looked around with shocked eyes.

"My God," he said. "Why did they pick *my* cottage?"

"They heard of it through Manette Venus," Walsh said. "It's one of those things."

188

"Look at this damage," Boothbay shouted. "Who's going to pay for it?"

Sergeant Beaupré said, "Maybe you can collect from the Yekiti estate."

"You're not being funny, are you?" Boothbay said sharply. "Some of this damage is due to the police."

"The sergeant was only joking," Walsh said. "If you want to make a claim to the Commonwealth, have your lawyer contact the attorney-general."

"I'll put in a claim for the entire cottage," Boothbay said. "I couldn't use this place any more. There were two men killed in here, weren't there?"

"Not in here," Walsh said. "They were shot outside. Mr. Boothbay, is that your Winchester rifle there?"

"No," Boothbay said emphatically.

"The Colt automatic?"

"I never owned a weapon in my life." He craned his neck, looking at the kitchen. "They cleaned out my refrigerator, too. Filthy animals. The place looks worse than a pigsty."

"It takes all kinds to make a world," Walsh said briskly. "Okay, Beaupré. Wrap it up. I want to get a normal duty roster working again."

CHAPTER 20 _____

THEY brought Calvaris from the cellblock and into the guardroom. Sergeant Stan Maleski sat him in a chair and gave him a cigarette. Then they ranged around him. Captain Walsh, Detective-Lieutenant Chet Granger, Captain Angsman, and the Danford Chief of Police. Kerrigan and I were there as door guards.

Granger was doing the interrogation. "What was the plan?" he asked Calvaris.

"We didn't have no plan no more," Calvaris said. "We had to beat it when Helen got knocked off."

"Why didn't you pull it anyway?"

"We couldn't get to our stuff in the warehouse. We figured we'd run into a stake-out."

"What was the original plan?" Granger asked.

"It was gonna be next Friday," Calvaris said, his sharp, unshaven face turning from one to the other. "The Staley Woolen Company. We had these funny masks and the smoke bombs and the guns. We wait until the armored truck drops the payroll and takes off. Then we go in."

"Who was to take the gate guard?" Granger asked.

"Me. They let me off first. I'm hanging around the gate like I'm looking for a job. Yekiti and Horace wait in the car down the road. I walk in and talk to the guard in the booth. Then I put the slug on him, tape him up and dump him on the floor. The car comes up quick. I stay in the booth and keep the gate clear. Yekiti and Horace go in and hit the office."

"How?"

"Up the side fire escape. The fire door on the second floor is gonna be open for them. There's a payola there."

"A payoff?"

"Yeah. Yekiti got to some dame in the office. She'd take care of the door."

"Just one girl?"

"Yeah."

"Nobody else? A man named Reece?"

"No."

"What was the girl's name?"

Calvaris shook his head. "I don't know nothing about the inside setup. Yekiti told us nothing about it."

"What was your cut in this?" Granger asked.

"Five grand."

"That all? The take was supposed to be two hundred grand."

"You're riding me," Calvaris said. "The take was gonna be about twenty-five big ones."

"Not twenty-five grand," Granger said. "Two hundred thousand."

"Yekiti wouldn't cross me," Calvaris said stubbornly.

"Why not?" Captain Walsh interrupted harshly. "He'd cross the devil himself. And so would you, Calvaris. And so would every one of you."

"Who was going to drive the getaway car?" Granger asked.

"Yekiti was gonna do all the driving."

"Where were you going to get a car?"

"We'd grab one somewhere. Horace was gonna do it."

Angsman moved in. "How about the route, Dick?"

"Al's got it all taped. We already run the route maybe five, six times in Al's car. We got it down perfect."

"When did you plan to switch cars?" Granger asked.

"Two miles down Route 7. There's a cutoff. Al's car is there. We get in it and go straight for the shack on Deer Pond. We stay there until the heat cools off. Then we split."

"You wouldn't go back to Danford?" Captain Angsman asked.

"Naw. We get paid off in the cottage. Then everybody splits up."

"What else?" Granger asked. "What were the smoke bombs for?"

"For the office," Calvaris explained. "We throw 'em. Make a lot of smoke. Nobody's gonna see a thing, 'specially the guard inside the building."

"What else?"

"That's all I know, Lieutenant."

"You're a liar, Dick," Granger said evenly. "Why did you kill Helen Toledo?"

"Me?" Calvaris asked with an injured look on his face. "I got nothing to do with that, Lieutenant."

"I got a mind to put my fist right through your teeth," Angsman said. "You were in the car when she was shot."

"So help me," Calvaris said earnestly. "I didn't know Al was gonna kill her."

"No?" Granger asked. "Then why were you waiting outside the hotel?"

"Al tells me there's a kid trooper who rides near the mill. He's supposed to be fixed. The fix fell through. Helen was supposed to set it up again. We were waiting outside to see how she made out. We wasn't gonna do nothing."

"You were waiting outside the hotel with a Schmeisser machine pistol. You were going to do nothing?"

"No, no," Calvaris said frantically. "Not me. Al Yekiti had the burp gun. We were only waiting outside to see what's gonna happen. Then this kid comes out and he's holding onto Helen and she's crying. So we know Helen's been pinched."

"So you decided to kill her," Granger said.

"No, no," Calvaris pleaded. He looked up at Granger and tugged at his coat sleeve. "You got it wrong, Lieutenant. Al tells us if the kid gets Helen to the barracks, she'll talk. She'll spill the whole operation. He says he's gonna get her. I figure he means a snatch, nothing more. I'm behind the wheel of the car, motor running, ready to go. Then Al starts to shoot the burp gun. I'm screaming at him, 'What's the idea?' Then I gun the car and get the hell out of there. I didn't know Al was gonna knock her off. So help me. You could ask Horace."

"Horace is dead," Granger said.

"You got to believe me, Lieutenant," Calvaris said, twisting his hands in his lap. "I didn't know Al was gonna kill anybody. That's the big rap. I never went for a deal like that."

"No?" Granger said. "Then what about Manette Venus?"

"I don't know nothing about her. Sure, I seen in the papers where some dame by that name got knocked off. I never heard of her before. You ain't gonna pin every killing in town on me, are you?"

"Didn't Yekiti ever mention Manette Venus to you?"

"No."

"You didn't know she was the girl planted inside the Staley office?"

"No. So help me. I didn't know nothing."

"Didn't Helen Toledo talk about Manette Venus?"

"Not to me. I steer clear of Helen all the time. Once I made a play for her and Al got sore and almost busted my back. So Helen and I stay far away."

"Did you ever hear of a state trooper named Ralph Lindsey?"

"I seen in the papers where he was mixed up with the Venus dame. But I don't know him."

"You see those two troopers standing at the door? One of them is Lindsey."

Calvaris peered at Kerrigan and me. He shook his head. "I don't know which one."

"The one on the left is Lindsey. He was with Helen Toledo when she was killed."

"It was dark and he was wearing regular clothes then. I didn't get a good look at him."

"Didn't you know Lindsey was the trooper who had the patrol near the factory?"

"Yekiti didn't tell us no names. I once seen a cruiser go by there. But Al says not to worry. He's gonna get it fixed."

"Why did you pick the cottage at Deer Pond for the hideout?"

194

"We got to get off the road fast. The state cops would be watching everywhere."

"But why *that* cottage?"

"Yekiti says it's a laugh. The cottage belongs to a guy who works in the woolen company. After the job is pulled, the guy's gonna be busy like a one-armed paper hanger. He's gonna be so tied up with the cops and mill bosses, he's gonna have no chance of coming out there. Me, I think it's a good rib. Who's gonna think of looking for us there?"

"Did you know the name of the man who owned the cottage?"

"I seen his name in the shack. Bootmaker or something."

"Boothbay," Granger said. "Cole Boothbay."

"Yeah, Boothbay. I seen him there talking to the cops."

"And you never saw him before that?"

"No, sir. That was the first time."

Granger went over and huddled with Walsh, Angsman and the Danford Chief of Police. He came back to Calvaris and said, "All right, you can go back to your cell. We'll talk to you later, when the D. A. gets here."

Calvaris stood up and rubbed his eyes. "Say," he said. "You sure the take was gonna be two hundred grand?"

"That's right," Granger said.

"So Yekiti was gonna cross us up," Calvaris sneered. "The big, big brain."

Sergeant Maleski, standing by, saw Granger nod. He took Calvaris by the arm and brought him back to the cell-block. I went with him. When the big steel barred door clanged shut, I saw Granger had left the guardroom. He was standing in the corridor. He motioned to me. I walked with him toward the dining room.

"I'm not sure," he said, "if we have the whole story."

195

"You don't think Calvaris was telling the truth?"

"I think he was. He has to save his own neck. But we never found that twin Colt."

"Yekiti could have tossed it away."

"Maybe. But I'm still wondering where Fulton Reece fits in."

"He killed himself so he wouldn't be questioned further," I said. "I don't know of a stronger admission of guilt, sir—"

"Reece was sick in the head," Granger said. "He could have killed himself because he was tired of fighting the world. In his own mind, he might have had a dozen reasons. Who knows?" He stopped and thrust his hands deep into his pockets. "Then I'm not sure we have a true picture of Manette Venus, either. I've got a feeling she was pushed into this against her will."

"Yes," I said. "But how?"

"I don't know yet. But we'll find out. The girl started in the operation. Then she wanted out. Maybe because she met you."

"But she was *supposed* to meet me. That was part of their plan."

"But she wasn't supposed to fall in love with you. When that happened, she tried to take you out of it. When she couldn't get you to leave the job she was going to tell you everything. Remember she promised to?"

"Yes," I said slowly.

"They knew it. They had to kill her first. Didn't you know the girl fell in love with you?"

"I had an idea," I said. "But I wasn't sure."

"I don't think you know too much about girls, kid. She wanted to go away with you, didn't she?"

196

"Yes, but I thought she wanted to get out of town, and she needed me for protection of some kind."

"I think she wanted to get *you* out of town, Ralph." He leaned against the wall. "It's too bad she didn't tell us sooner. We could have done something for her then. It leaves a bad taste with me."

"She wasn't a bad person," I said thoughtfully. I turned to him. "Was she bad, Lieutenant?"

He came away from the wall. "No," he said. "I think she got tangled up somewhere and couldn't get free."

He left me then. He went into the duty office. I could hear him calling the district attorney.

CHAPTER 21 _____

AFTER lunch I phoned my father in Cambridge. I asked about Ellen and he said she was home. The Levesques had been in to see him and there had been some tears and, at least, *he* had been forgiven. I told him my day off was starting at five in the afternoon, but I had a short patrol to do first.

I was restless. I had a half-hour before I went on patrol. There was something gnawing inside me. The picture didn't fit and all the ends weren't tied and Lieutenant Granger knew it, too. I paced the empty guardroom. Then I went into the communications room and watched the teletype machines. After a moment the steady sound of the machines bothered me. I started to go out.

The dispatcher called me. "Weren't you working on the Venus case?" he asked.

"Yes," I said.

"There's a TT here from the New York police. Maybe you're interested."

I took the perforated paper and looked at it. It was information on the Signet Crest Company. It reported that the firm was a mail-drop house.

"Can I have the blue sheet?" I asked.

"Sure," he said. He gave me the blue copy. I took it and went into the duty office. I put it on Sergeant Maleski's desk. He read it.

"So what?" he said.

"What's a mail-drop house?"

"An address," Maleski said. "A hole in the wall. They charge so much a month. You have your mail sent there. They forward it to you wherever you are. They remail letters for you from their address."

"What's the purpose?"

"Some people want a New York address. They try to put up a front. They might be making phony deals and corresponding with people and they don't want anybody to know where they really are. A lot of phony stuff is pulled that way. Some of these mail drops are used by men on the run. Ex-cons and sharpshooters use them. A few of these outfits are crooked and they'll furnish you with any kind of job history and references you want. For a price, that is."

"Thanks," I said slowly.

I went out. So there it was. Everything. I knew it would be a matter of seconds before the teletype message was relayed to GHQ in Boston. It would be a matter of minutes before Ed Newpole saw it and began to move. And I knew I had to move first. I had gotten into it myself and I had to finish it myself—for my own peace of mind.

Because everything dovetailed now. The Staley Woolen

holdup had been scheduled for next Friday and the plan was going through even after Manette Venus had been killed. Because someone else was still planted in the Staley Woolen office to open the fire door for Yekiti and his gang. And it was the person who had planned the entire thing. Not the slow-witted Al Yekiti, or the troubled, inadequate Fulton Reece. But Manette's ex-husband. A man named Andrew Fleer.

I ran down the corridor buckling on my service belt. At the door leading downstairs to the garage, I bumped into Phil Kerrigan coming in.

"Hi." He grinned. "What's the hurry, kid?"

"I've got a patrol," I said.

He looked at his wrist watch. "You've got fifteen minutes yet, haven't you?"

"No, I've no time at all," I said. "I'll see you, Phil."

I ran out. I brought the cruiser around, turned onto the turnpike and sped off toward Staleyville.

I drove in through the gate of the Staley Woolen Company, past the aged guard, and parked in front of the office building. I went inside. I was hoping he still felt safe and secure, that he was still there.

He was. Cole Boothbay was sitting behind his desk. I went straight to the counter. He looked up and saw me. He rose up and sauntered over.

"I've come to take you in, Fleer," I said to him.

"What?" he asked.

"I'm taking you in, Fleer."

His eyebrows came up. "Fleer? Who are you talking to?"

200

"You. Andrew Fleer. The husband of Margaret Fleer, Manette Venus, Margaret Venable. Take your pick."

He had a maddening, supercilious smile. "Take my pick? Take yourself out of here, Lindsey. I hardly knew the girl."

"You were married to her. Your real name is Andrew Fleer."

"Oh, is it? My name is Cole Boothbay. I've worked here a year. Check the record. Before that, I was with Signet Crest five years. Pick up a phone and call them. They'll verify it."

"No good," I said. "Signet Crest is a mail-drop house. We'll have your prints and pictures from Chicago by telephoto in an hour. You going to quibble about something we'll know in an hour?"

Fleer looked down at the counter. He spread his hands flat. "You know," he said softly, "I think you mean it."

"Your name is Fleer, isn't it?"

He looked up with bright eyes. "Why get all excited, Lindsey? So what? I served my time in Illinois. You've got nothing on me."

"There was a conspiracy to commit armed robbery at Staley Woolen," I said. "I don't know how far back you planned it. Maybe when you first came here. You used to watch them bring in the payroll every Friday. It struck you that, with a little help, the job could be pulled. You needed a couple of dumb gunmen to take orders. And you bought the cottage at Deer Pond for a hideaway. But you needed a girl, too."

He laughed in my face. "Why would I need a girl?"

"You'd watch the road from the window every Friday morning. After the payroll truck left there'd be a State Police cruiser outside the gate. But each time the cruiser would come from a different direction. Someone had to get that trooper out of the way. Margaret could."

"That's fine logic," he said. "And how would I get hold of her? She divorced me. She left Chicago. How would I know where she was?"

"You found out. You trailed her to Cleveland, where she was living. It was easy. She wasn't a criminal. She didn't know how to cover her tracks well. Not like you could."

"But you're contradicting yourself," Fleer said. "If she wasn't a criminal, she wouldn't come in on any deal, would she?"

"She had no choice. There was a warrant still out against her for the first job you pulled. She didn't want to be sent back to Chicago."

"You think I threatened her with that?"

"Yes. You forced her to come in. Maybe you told her it was just this once, then you'd let her go."

"You think you've sized me up pretty good, don't you, Lindsey?"

I shook my head. "I haven't bothered to size you up at all, Fleer. You're a sharpshooter, an angle boy. You were even going to clip the gunmen who were doing the actual work."

"All I've heard so far," Fleer said, "is mention of a hold-up-to-be. No holdup ever took place. So you have no evidence against me. No man can be arrested for thinking."

"For conspiracy he can," I said. "And also for murder. You knew Manette was going to expose the whole job. You went over to Glen Road and killed her."

"I had an idea somebody else killed her," he said distantly. His hands dropped behind the counter. "But they released Ellen Levesque. Why?"

202

"Because it was the wrong gun. There was another .32-20 Colt. There was a pair of them. Manette had one. You, her ex-husband, had the other."

"So you're here to arrest me for Margaret's murder," he said.

"Yes," I said.

"You came alone. You're going to make a big grandstand play by bringing me in."

"Not a grandstand play," I said heavily. "A man can't pass the buck. He has to straighten out his own problems. This thing started with me. It has to finish with me. A man's got to live with himself a long time."

"How long are you going to live?" he asked gently. His hand came up from behind the counter. In it was the pearl-handled revolver. "Is this the gun you were looking for?" he asked.

"Yes," I said slowly.

"And what are you going to do about it, Lindsey?"

I did nothing. I said nothing. My hands hung limp. Fleer backed away from the counter, the gun pointed at me. The girls in the office began to squeal in terror. They were leaving their desks and huddling in the back of the room.

"I'd like to give it to you, Lindsey," he said between his teeth. "Here and now. So don't tempt me."

One girl behind him seemed stupefied. She had stood up at her desk, faltered, and was unable to move. Fleer reached out and grabbed her. She was a short, thin brunette with wide, panic-stricken eyes. Fleer held her wrist. He pulled her in front of him.

"Five minutes," he said to me in a squeezed voice. "I need five minutes to get away. If not, I'll kill her. And you know I'll kill her. Five minutes, Lindsey."

He backed up, pulling the girl with him. He brought the gun up and held the muzzle to the girl's neck. The girl's mouth opened spasmodically but no sound came. Her knees started to buckle. Fleer put his arm around her and held her up.

I began to edge for the counter gate. "Where can you go?" I asked him harshly.

"Five minutes," Fleer said, his voice taut. He kept backing. He half-dragged the girl as he moved for the fire door. I opened my holster flap and brought out the service revolver. I started to bring it up.

"I said I'd kill her," he said, soft-voiced. "Move away from the gate, Lindsey."

I backed away, the gun hanging loosely in my hand.

Fleer was up against the fire door now, the girl in front of him. The other girls, screaming, had skittered away from the door and were hiding behind the desks. Fleer reached behind him, fumbled with the lock of the door, and opened it. He moved back on the fire escape, gingerly, feeling his way, dragging the girl with him. The door slammed shut.

I ran. I clattered down the front stairs and outside. I started for the rear of the building with my gun cocked. But around the edge of it, instead of Fleer, the girl's nyloned leg and skirt came into view. He was crouched behind her.

"Get back," he shouted at me. He saw the cruiser. He lifted his gun and fired at the front of it, the bullet whacking into the radiator. He moved along, shielding himself with the girl. There was a gray convertible parked twenty feet away. He opened the door and backed in crabwise. He dragged the girl in behind him. He started the motor. The car swung around. The gate guard, who had heard the shot,

204

was outside his shack, looking with bewilderment. The gray convertible swept by him. As it went through the gate opening and turned onto the road, I jumped for the cruiser.

I started it. I went through the gate and turned out after him. I had one hand on the wheel. The other hand was holding the radiophone. I called Troop E. I gave them the name, description and registration number of the convertible. I told them he was traveling south on Route 7, that he had kidnapped a girl and that he was armed.

He was ahead of me a quarter of a mile by now. I pushed the gas pedal down to the floor. The cruiser bucked and raced forward. But his car was fast. I saw steam beginning to wreathe around the hood of the cruiser. There was a smell of heat. His bullet had done damage. The motor began to skip and the steam thickened. Globs of water were hitting the windshield. The cruiser was coughing, slowing and falling back. We came to a hill and went over the crest of it. The distance was widening between us.

A half-mile straight ahead there was a route junction. I saw a pale-blue cruiser move across it and block the road. The gray convertible slowed, swerved onto the dirt shoulder of the road and skidded to a stop. The door opened and Fleer ran out. He slithered down the embankment. I drove up and jammed on the brakes. I was out of the car fast. I ran by the convertible, took one quick look, and saw the girl huddled, bug-eyed, in the front seat. I went over the embankment.

It was a field. The grass was high. I saw him running across it. I heard a siren whining in the distance. I stumbled through the high brown grass after him. He turned and fired twice at me. Haphazardly and frantically. His shots were wide.

He came to a stone wall, waist-high. He vaulted over it and disappeared. There he stayed. I moved up, my gun still by my side. His head bobbed up from behind the wall. He took two more shots at me and missed. He ducked again. I was walking slowly now. He was only ten feet away.

"You've got one round left," I called to him. "Use it."

There was no answer from him. I couldn't see him behind the wall. I moved the ten yards, came to the wall and stopped. I brought up my gun. My shoe was prodding the chinks of stone for a foothold.

"Hold it," Fleer shouted. "Don't, Lindsey. See? I'm throwing away the gun. I'm unarmed." The pearl-handled revolver came twinkling over the wall and dropped at my feet. I kicked it away.

"Stand up," I said. "With your hands behind your head."

He stood up, breathing rapidly, his breath wheezing. His fingers were laced in back of his head. I opened my handcuff case. I half-turned. On the road I saw two more cruisers parked. In the field, running toward us, were Hank Ravelli and Manny Green.

Ravelli came up first. He grabbed Fleer, twisted him around, and took the handcuffs from me. He locked Fleer's arms behind his back.

"You had a chance to shoot him," Ravelli said to me. "Manny and I were afraid you—"

"I know," I said bitterly. "And I was thinking about it, too."

CHAPTER 22 _____

WHEN I drove home to Cambridge I saw a black Mercury in front of our house. I knew it was Captain Walsh's. I came inside and kissed my mother.

"Where are they?" I asked.

"On the sun porch," my mother said. "Captain Walsh is discussing something with your father."

I went out there. They were looking at a page of notes. When my father saw me he put his pencil down. He said, "What do you think, Ralph? We're going to write a book."

"A book?" I asked. "What kind of a book, Pa?"

"A sort of history of the State Police," my father said. "It's going to keep me pretty busy. It was Captain Walsh's idea."

"A man needs a hobby," Walsh said. "And I don't know of anybody who's more qualified to do a history of the S. P."

"We can get a lot of stuff from the state archives," my

father said. "In the old days," he continued reminiscently, "they called them the state constabulary. They rode horses then."

"Which was before my time," Walsh said to me. "But when I get through next spring, I can help your father with it."

"You, sir?" I said.

"Why not?" Walsh said. "I've only got a few more months to go. I might as well start planning now. I can do the leg work, and go out and interview all the old-timers. I'd enjoy that." He stopped and looked at his watch. "I have to go now. I've got to inspect a couple of substations." He went to the doorway. He turned. "I'll tell you right in front of him, Walt," he said to my father. "You've got a good boy. He'll make out fine. If he don't get court-martialed first, he'll end up as executive officer or captain-adjutant. You'll see."

I said, "Thank you, sir. I'm trying to make all my mistakes now."

"We never stop making mistakes," Walsh said. "But as long as they're honest ones we get by. While I'm here, I might as well tell you, Ralph. You've got an extra day off. Don't report back until Saturday night."

"Thanks, sir," I said.

"You did wrong in going after Fleer without orders. If you'd lost him, you'd have been discharged immediately. You know that now, don't you?"

"Yes, sir."

"Did you know it when you went after him?"

"Yes, sir."

"You brought him in. So I had no choice but to give you a day off. But I wouldn't try it again. The Commonwealth spent too much money training you and I'd hate to take your badge away. Good-by, Walt. I'll call you."

He went out. I looked at my father. There was a smile on his face. "You can't say Fred isn't fair," he said. "But what are you wasting time around here for? Ellen is home."

"Ellen doesn't want to see me."

"For a tough cop, you're a lot of mush when it comes to girls. How do you know she doesn't want to see you?"

"She let me know, all right."

"Look, when I was courting your mother—" He stopped and shook his head. "No, no more stories. I just say a man doesn't know until he tries."

So I went over to Ellen's house. She answered the door herself. She was wearing a new dress with a flared skirt and her shoes had high heels.

"If I'm not welcome," I said, "you can shut the door quick."

She kept it open. "I was waiting for you," she said. "You've been home ten minutes. But it seems like hours since your car drove up."

"If I had known—" I started to say.

"Oh, there are so many things you don't know. You're the biggest hick in the world, sometimes. Let's go for a walk."

She stepped outside. We went down the stairs and walked along the sidewalk. I scuffed at the leaves.

"I was over to your house before," she said. "I was talking to Captain Walsh. He's a real grizzly bear, isn't he?"

I grinned. "Hard but fair, as my father always says."

"And sensible, too. We were talking about how a man selects his company and how it shows his true character.

209

Then we talked about Manette Venus. You still insist she wasn't a bad girl, don't you?"

"Yes," I said.

The breeze whipped at her black hair. She pushed a wisp away from her freckled little nose. "That Andrew Fleer," she said. "He married Manette when she was only eighteen. She'd never been away from Ames, Iowa. He brought her to Chicago. I'll bet anything she didn't know what he was doing when he tried that blackmail thing."

"Most likely not."

"After she divorced him, she ran away and hid in Cleveland under an assumed name. But she didn't know how to hide. He found her. He forced her to contact you, to pick you up. I kept thinking what a sap you were to fall for it. But you weren't a sap. She was a nice girl, wasn't she?"

"Yes, but not as—"

"I know." She smiled. "You're going to say she wasn't as nice as me. She probably was, maybe nicer. You wouldn't know in such a short time. Anyway, I'm sorry I was so thick-headed about it. Or would you call it bad-tempered?"

"Quick-tempered," I corrected. "And I like it on you. It's part of you and I'm used to it."

We kept walking. She said, "Manette must have loved you a great deal. Perhaps I sensed it and that's why I was so jealous. But don't be too hard on me. I made plans to marry you a long, long time ago."

"Then as long as we're talking about it," I said, "let's follow through."

"That's what I was leading up to so subtly," she said, smiling mischievously. "But don't hand me generalities, trooper. I can be tough too. Lay it on the line. When?"

"I don't know." I grinned. "I thought the girl usually set the date."

"Then you've made a deal," she said. "You'd better be ready in thirty days, morning suit, ring, best man, and all. Okay?"

"Okay."

She stopped. "Well?"

I stopped. "Well, what?"

She sighed. "At least," she said, "you could kiss me."

"I was thinking the same thing," I said. "But here? In the middle of the street?"

"Here," she said firmly. "So pucker up, trooper."